The Owner of Lido

The Owner of Lido

Nikos Grego

To my cousin Anthony

One

Kasos island, *Dodecanese*

The lamp had gone out for hours and this helped the cigarette burn to illuminate a part of his face and his uncovered forehead, the beautiful lines of the almond-shaped eyes, and the thick eyebrows that curved around them. The long lashes on the edges of the prominent cheekbones, the curtain of the thick, perfectly trimmed mustache and the thin mouth, slightly higher than the dark brown lapels of the *robe de chambre*, were mysteriously portrayed. The dim light, reciprocating periodically, made in that same eerie way his fingers and the ashtray visible. He sat in the dark living room, the largest of the three rooms upstairs, with the large table and six chairs in the middle of the floor, the oblong sofa neatly oriented beside them.

His chair, pulled just enough to give him the necessary space, stood out from the others which were carefully resting on the perimeter of the table. The shutters of the balcony door were locked against the sleeping sunrise, just as he remembered leaving them last time. The other two rooms, facing directly and at the greatest possible distance from the balcony door, were the small bedrooms. A wooden staircase led to the ground-floor. There, the kitchen with the built-in oven and the marble trough, the relatively spacious dining room with the six tall wooden seats and the round table, the indoor toilet, the warm in winters and cool in summers habitat, gave a sense of pure luxury. The two-story house, dowry of his wife and one of the most beautiful mansions on the island, surrounded him protectively like a shell.

But the luster of the island, now hidden behind the heavy cloak of the night and the smoke of his cigarette, was frayed in the eyes of his frightened soul. He hated it! Ever since he was a child, when he first went with his father to *Alexandria*, he felt the warmth of the big city like an imprisoned animal finally released. The myriad people with the strange dresses and the incomprehensible speech, the huge streets with all kinds of shops, the smells—he had come to the interesting conclusion that there was something completely different about this very air of *Egypt*—managed unceremoniously to change his way of life.

A life that his father made sure to make as comfortable as possible from the beginning by stepping on the solid foundations of his professional identity, whose managerial post in the admirable field of engineering—in the construction of the *Suez* Canal—ensured the conditions for success. Proof of this success was the small three-story building on the land of the *Pharaohs*, the apartments of which he rented, 'for a convenient interest,' to the *Egyptians*.

His good father! A man who inspired respect in anyone who came close to his sphere of influence and who used to say to him, sitting behind his desk with his hands forming a protective semicircle, like a small hug over the drawings, pencils, erasers and other objects that adorned the anarchically laden furniture: "We must respect foreigners! Here are the *French*, say, who give us jobs. The *English*! All the people without discrimination. Because, don't forget, we too are foreigners in this land..." Managing to impart to him this respect for "foreigners" but failing, fortunately, to convey to him the instinctive racism he felt for the locals, whom *Nikolas* fairly counted as his brothers.

The larger apartment on the ground floor had been converted into a tailor's shop, the pretext for his son's *professional status*. Not because the young man desired it or indicated it to him in one way or another, but because he believed that this inspiration had a better chance of success than any other choice; because he wanted to help him, to push him forward, seeing the difficulties and his hesitant steps to move in the right direction. For, apart from the island, his son hated work as well. Not only his own, but any kind of occupation, even if it involved something like, shall we say, artistic, where he had no inclination whatsoever. Thus, while he would touch the various fabrics at the first opportunity and look at them in the light as if he were himself a great dressmaker, in reality he trusted the business to two or three local tailor assistants, who even took care of the marketing of the products.

He had learned the 'art' in *Athens*. In a narrow alley perpendicular to *Ermou Street* was, as he said, without much arrogance, if one excluded the natural interest in promoting the qualities of the new profession, addressing his father or his friends to inform them: "the school of sewing". Next to the school, the small *café* was his consolation. His favorite *café*, where every morning he would enjoy hot beverages or a few drops of *strong cognac*, light his cigarette and forget that his colleagues were leaning over the colorful fabrics and carefully cut patterns with the passion of the creator.

Over the round table two or three, and often more idlers, would hang out with him. The low-pitched speeches, mingling with the random noises from the adjacent tables—the rustling of a chair, the claps of crockery, the sudden laughter of a patron, the view outside the huge windows that started almost from the floor and reached almost to the ceiling, the passers-by walking on the sidewalk—calmed his naïve soul. To take over the endless conversations and spicy stories that would quickly bring him joy, release the desire to transmit this mood to others, make him raise his glass high with increasing frequency and drink to their health with authentic greed. And late in the afternoon, when his classmates had long since gone to their homes, he would walk among the sewing machines, look indifferently at the unfinished patterns, and, on leaving, pat the doorman's back amicably, whistling some cheerful melody or reciting loudly—his voice was characteristically thunderous but without much musical sense—the lyrics of a song he happened to hear the night before: "I don't care, my lady, I don't care, what will people say!"

And it was true that he married very young. As it was true that the long shadows, the late shadows of this act, often occupied his thoughts, managing to penetrate the thin curtain of the past time and the smoke from the cigarettes he smoked. Yes, he married young, just like someone looking away and stumbling upon a pole that suddenly sprang up in the middle of the sidewalk. He could not see then that the blow would be fatal, not for him but for his wife. After the birth of his second daughter, the unfortunate mother suffered ... how did the doctors say it? The words, whenever this subject tormented him, came to his mind cut off, one after the other, cold, as they were said on the lips of indifferent medics—like stamps of post office employees on lifeless envelops: 'black-melancholy' 'coldness' 'postpartum depression' ... A young priest-doctor from *Cairo* even mentioned the word 'vampire!' The sympathetic servants of medicine had warned him that he should not, for any reason, have a third child. And *Nikolas* had tried, unsuccessfully, to heed their advice, leaving her for long periods of time 'on the island' 'to her own people' 'for her own good...' As he briefly stated, without any distinction at all, but even to deceive himself, to appease his guilty conscience—making his life in the city he loved, wasting the money he earned with incredible recklessness, leaving only their imprints in his drawers on the dust that covered them.

But memory, like the footprints of dust in his drawers, insisted on pushing its probes on the most sensitive corners of his soul. It brought together, especially here, on the island where he was born, the events that marked his life and family. The street that had the honor of being called *Arais Street* and on which stood the three-story apartment building he inherited from his father. He remembered the comment his sister had made on the second floor of this apartment building, just above the tailor's shop: "Well, that *molokhia* broth tastes amazing!" she said, addressing aunt *Joanna*, because she admired the way she cooked. Yes, he was absolutely certain that his sister admired the countrywoman's abilities and that she was not at all ashamed to admit it. They sat around the large dining room table—on the one hand, the three children, with him, along with aunt *Joanna* and on the other, *Evangelia* his sister along with her husband *Georgios Demestichas*.

His sister had had a very good marriage, "the best wedding in the whole of *Alexandria*!" as it was whispered to this day, secretly and openly, even in front of her. And this he knew satisfied her deeply, it certainly amused her immeasurably. But he felt, at the same time, that she was jealous of her husband's bizarre devotion to the underground corridors of endless rows of barrels, the unpainted walls with the successive hanging of bottles—that she hated even the dedication of the employees who affixed the painted labels, "always performing the same movements without lifting their heads for a moment to see a little farther from the point of the dull object of their work." Besides, she had confided to him that she felt uncomfortable in the winery: "It's like another woman is among us," she had told him, looking at him in the familiar haughty way that was perfectly in harmony with the imperial way she posed her huge body.

That night his son-in-law had tried to cheer him up by urging him to taste the wine, but he had failed because he did not know that his spirit was fluttering elsewhere. The death of his wife, the debts piling up around his neck, the future of his children, and his own that looked like a bottomless precipice beneath his feet, may not have given any hope to his wealthy relative by marriage, but they did not prevent him from dreaming of the places where he had been proclaimed king. Yes, his spirit fluttered in the dark halls of nightclubs. And that night was no exception. His soul fluttered to the rhythms of their lustful music that helped him, even when he was away from these "charitable institutions," to move forward in the rough terrain of everyday life.

But he was vulnerable and defenseless against his eldest daughter. His *sparkling star*, who had enthusiastically accepted his sister's invitation, smiling, without taking a glance at him to see how happy he was with her joy. His beloved child, who wore a black blouse that made the transparent shades of her face visible in the contrast of the dark lines of her thin eyebrows, and long eyelashes, the pulled back hair, highlighting the unparalleled and aggressively provocative beauty of her body and physiognomy. Yes, that is exactly how he remembered her when he closed the door behind her to escort her relatives down to the carriage, where old *Abdul* waited patiently, mounted on the seat of the small but luxurious means of transport—like a cry of triumph under the starry sky, in the autumn air around the lanterns of the carriage, which would fade after a while at the first turn of the thoroughfare.

Two

Alexandria, January 1921

The owner of the *Lido* nightclub never slept before noon. When the last customer left, this dignified and important gentleman retired unswervingly to the small room that communicated directly with the guichet of the business, holding tightly in the protection of his bosom—with both arms crossed forming a prohibitive 'X'—the leather bag with the earnings of the 'day'. There, isolated like a snail in its shell, turning the switch that supplied electricity to the lamp of the ceiling, he emptied the contents of the bag onto the largest of the three pieces of furniture.

The *décor* included a wooden desk and two comfortable armchairs—lined with expensive fabric: 'for *agents* and *impresarios*', but 'for friends' as well who had a complaint or would be prone to discuss something 'particularly interesting' with him. In this small space, sitting with his body stretched like the bow of an archer, his head slightly tilted, he would start counting. He always counted three and four times, for verification, noting the result each time in a thick notebook. When the result was exactly the same in the successive amounts, he would tie the notes in a bunch, separating the coins in the desk drawer, get up and place the bunch in the hidden safe. The walls of the small room, full of photographs and posters of "artistic" content, glued one on top of the other, hid the whole story of success.

This morning, having finished the "holy" count, visibly satisfied with the result, he paced slowly between the empty tables, spinning incessantly in his right hand an amber rosary. In the silence that reigned in the great hall, the beads rattled so clearly that he could measure them by the sound: 'tack, tack, tack! one, two, three!' Counting was his great weakness. The tables, for example, one hundred in number for years, he counted them at every opportunity and despite the simplicity of the equation, since four chairs corresponded to each one easily giving the result of the number four hundred, he always insisted on the certainty of his primitive method. Sitting or standing, or pacing, as happened to happen now between them, he would count them with the same reverence that ants follow each other to find their way to their nest: 'one, two, three!'—as if he wanted to prove the solidity of the floor beneath the steady gait of his patent leather shoes.

With the years weighing on his square shoulders as much as half the tables in the spacious room, he was a man of dark complexion and of average stature and so square in overall construction that proportions lost their importance in his case. Without being particularly stout, with thick short-cut raven black hair and no trace of white from one end of the head to the other. His square face, in harmony with the outline of his body, projected a strong nose and rich mustache above the intensely willful chin, in contrast to his well-shaved skin. His eyes, black and bright, let the energy of his soul run free to overwhelm the unsuspecting observer. Alone in life, the need to set his feet as firmly as possible on the earth had pushed him down paths where the words 'money', 'interest', 'banker' were by no means unknown. The word 'banker' in particular flattered him like nothing else in the world and, although he hated the euphemism *'loan shark'* and could stab the first naïve person to utter the words, he took care to prove his love of the fancy title by lending money with great care. First to 'friends and acquaintances' and then to 'complete strangers,' for whom of course he first rushed to discreetly gather the 'necessary information'.

He could easily, and in fact did so very often as a kind of pleasant exercise close to his favorite count, 'list' to himself his 'distinguished clients'. Everyone's name, address, professional progress, masochistically focusing on repeating the most important peculiarities of their lives—such as, for example, their assets and the assets of their relatives. And, of course, the amounts owed to him individually, the exact dates of payments, the balances of money in the affairs of well-payers, without looking at the carefully and clearly written entries in his books insured in the safe.

It was precisely because of this capacity, but also as an owner of a nightclub, that he had three henchmen in his service. People of his absolute trust, for whom, as he confided to the interested parties, immediately after the successful conclusion of an agreement, with the clear tones of his voice a little higher than normal, always in the singular for the benefit of intimacy and at the expense of politeness:

'From now on, my dear friend, you will only talk to good *Yusuf*!' Introducing the dark-skinned man with the unflappable face and arms crossed high on his chest, concluding meaningfully:

'Believe me my dear, I searched under every stone to find the right people! Believe me, my dear friend, they deserve, as you will soon value for yourself, the last shilling I spend on them!'

To the incessant 'tack, tack, tack', made by the beads of the amber rosary, the ringing of the bell that was hung above the front door was added suddenly. With his back turned to the entrance of the store, the piercing sound made him stop abruptly and rotate around his heels in a way reminiscent of a well-trained ballerina. The movement, intensely characteristic as well as improbable for the square construction of his inelegant body, was rather comical as the black suit, the leather vest visible through the jacket, the tight tie on the white shirt and the black shoes he wore, did not match a ballerina attire at all. But it was not noticed by the cleaner, who, opening the front door, focused her attention on the things she was carrying and that were necessary for her job.

Letting the bucket of her left hand rest on the floor, supporting her body with the other, using the broom pole as an aid to lift her from the crouched position, her gaze met the gaze of her patron. In her cloudy eyes gleamed a flash of fear, like the sudden flash of lightning that sweeps through the waves of the desolate sea at night as she greeted him in *Arabic*. Stoned in the same position, bowing and tilting her head again in respect, with all the power of her femininity hidden behind the headscarf and long desert-colored dresses, up to the gray sandals on her well-covered feet:

'Sabah elhir! Sabah elhir! Sabah—Sabah effendi!'

The owner of the *Lido*, apart from a nod to his head, did not deign to pay any other attention to the presence of the woman—whose silhouette, despite the neutral attire, would not be lost unnoticed in the general indifference of, say, the street market, or the busy streets of the big city, where the eyes have the opportunity to appreciate things other than the merchandise on the stalls or the ornate shop windows—and with the beads rattling again in his palm he continued to pace between the tables. In his mind, for a while now, the idea of a morning walk came and went. The nightclub was very close to the sea and its smell, which flooded the room at the door opening, along with the annoying noise made by the woman wiping the floor and moving the tables, resulted in his approaching the front door faster, reaching out his hand and opening it, decisively turning the golden-colored doorknob.

The sun had just risen and the huge disk in his right hand was casting its rays obliquely, breaking the light into countless reflections on the surface of the sea, causing him to half close his eyes. The brow of the shore bordering the sea was made of stone, more than one or two meters above the surface of the water, with a low wall at the edge of the curb—interrupted at regular points by narrow openings, like small gates to the stone stairs leading directly to the shallow seabed. Along the low wall there were oblong marble stalls on one of which he finally sat, having calculated that to go from one to the other needed exactly twenty steps. With this thought digesting in his idle mind, he slipped his free hand into the outer pocket of his jacket, only to display a pack of cigarettes immediately afterwards. From this position he continued and, tapping with his fingers on the bottom of the packet, singled out a cigarette inside. He lit it with a match that also appeared out of nowhere and, carefully putting the burnt match back into the package, withdrew it in the same way and in the same pocket of his jacket.

The smoke, along with the calm breathing of the sea, helped him relax in a few minutes so much so that the released fatigue found the opportunity to weigh down his eyelids pleasantly. In front of him stretched the wide road between the promenade, where he sat, and the row of shops, between which the *Lido* with its lights off looked abandoned and deserted. Low and oblong, like a perfect parallelogram, with the electric inscription off in the center just above the main entrance, its size was doubled by the shadow cast by the oblique rays of light, and this satisfied him, as every man pleases, the augmentation, even if illusory, of his power. For two or three minutes he almost fell asleep in the arms of the calm splashes, cigarette hanging from his lips, ready to fall at the first blow of the north wind and ash staining the well-ironed lapels of his flawless jacket.

Last night was a good night! Two exquisite girls from *France* made a special sensation in the shop, dangerously challenging the audience with their program. He wished he could keep them permanently, but that was impossible since the dancers from *Europe* did not stay for more than a month and their agents, taking advantage of the extremely strict *Egyptian* laws, made sure to move them in time. But how right are those who say that there is no more beautiful language than *French*! Especially when pronounced through such lips! Even this rocking womanlike, the stranded *French* agent with the floral shirt and long fingers, uttered the words so beautifully when presented the girls to him.

'Monsieur Michaëlis, regarder! C'est Vivi et c'est Natalie! C'est beau Vivi et c'est beau Natalie! Eh, regarder monsieur Michaëlis, eh!" He had stretched out his arms like a clown, palms spread, pointing to where the two girls were standing—tilting his lean body slightly against his fragile waist and long, equally thin legs, with his floral shirt completely out of his pantaloon. His fingers, long and erect, guided through the floral shirt, had continued for some time after the short speech to draw curved lines in the air, faithfully copying the curves of the bodies he displayed.

It was a very good night last night, yes, but some good and regular customers had many days to be seen, he thought, as he shook with his hand the ashes from the lapels of his jacket and the fabric of his pants. He had risen from the bench, continuing to shake off the ashes with one hand, twirling the rosary again in rhythm in the other, starting to pace the walk he intended to complete. *Nikolas* had days to show! This man, apart from being the tailor of the suit from which he now shook the ashes, was also the soul of the fun, a kind of attraction for his shop. Yes, that was true, although lately he had not been doing well financially at all, and so he had been added to his long list of books. An absolutely positive development in every respect. The amount was respectable, and he remembered *Nikolas'* look when asked: 'It's urgent, do you understand *Michael*? I have to pay my employees immediately! Must! I have no more room for maneuver...'

He had not preserved the continuation of the sentence, as the outstretched hand clasped his arm pleadingly. The details did not interest him at all, but he knew this look very well, he had seen it and seen it again countless times—as well as the pleading tone of voice, the confidential tightness of the man's fingers on his arm. What mattered was to attach another victim to the formidable chariot of this kind of power, to add another stone to the pillars of the sturdy edifice. And especially for *Nikolas*, being a friend and acquaintance, he had one more reason to desire his attachment. An absolutely positive development of things in every respect, yes!

He felt a euphoria starting from his feet, vibrating in their swift embrace of the hard ground, to the roots of his thick hair. *Nikolas* had a wonderful family and, although he had the misfortune of losing his wife very early, he had three children. Indeed, three children! He was jealous of him for that. And his eldest daughter, so beautiful! The dream of every father and every husband! Husband, truly yes, why not? He smiled internally at the idea, simultaneously slipping his hand into the outer pocket of his jacket, mechanically repeating the same sleight of hand, lighting a second cigarette, without interrupting the joyful rhythm of his gait. After a puff or two, he threw it, slamming it to the edge of the pavement. The cigarette smoke seemed suddenly unbearably annoying to him, made his tongue burn, brought to the mouth a sudden cough that forced him to stop.

For the first time since he got up from the curb-bench, he looked with some attention around him. Until now he had paid no attention to what was happening, or what was going through in front of his eyes. The boulevard was now busier. Full of passers-by with a specific purpose in their footsteps, it seemed to be brought to life by the sun, which, unhooked from the horizon, climbed into the sky. He did not recognize any of them out there, and that was perfectly normal, since his customers were not used to being on the road at that time. The landscape seemed completely alien to him, as he started again, regaining his rhythm, only to fade into oblivion in the first twists of the rosary.

He began counting his steps again: 'one, two, three!' coordinating the bead taps with them: 'tack, tack, tack!' Yet he did not want to risk a number because he did not like to fall out and then, yes, it was still quite far away! And as the sky, unlike the earth which embraced almost protectively the shaking of his feet, seemed not to exist for him above his head, so in his ears there was no sound other than that made by the beads, his eyes seeing only a few feet beyond his shoes. Like a powerful beast, not deigning to move its neck in any impending danger, he fearlessly moved straight ahead.

* * * * *

The night had passed quickly for the *Greek* tailor, who, sitting on the edge of the double bed in the middle of the small bedroom, kept his head resting between his two hands, trying to remember the nightmare that bowed for a while like a bright *harlequin* on the stage of a non-existent theater. Like a pebble disappearing in its contact with water, the *harlequin* had disappeared, leaving behind a tail of light, a series of impossible turbulences that were abruptly extinguished in an inexplicable way. The next moment, abandoning the hammock of this incredibly annoying and short break, putting the slippers on his feet, he had completely forgotten the strange experience of the bad dream. Before he turned to the bedroom door, *Joanna's* voice caught up with him:

'*Nikola*, eh *Nikola*, do you want coffee?'

He did not respond, knowing that this would be unnecessary. *Joanna* cried more so as not to let him sleep more than he should, and then coffee would be served even if he said no.

The hot coffee, drunk with small intermittent draughts through the porcelain cup, holding it with his fingertips as if it were the most precious jewel in the world, banished the last trace of sleep. Before he succeeded in putting it back on its saucer, he managed to bring the cigarette he had just lit with his other hand to his half-open mouth. The clock on the opposite wall struck half an hour. He turned and looked at it. Always soft-spoken, mornings were, however, the time he enjoyed more than any other, with the sole exception of moments of fun. When he said good morning for the second time he was already wearing his black everyday suit, ready to descend the external staircase that led to the ground floor. Before closing the door behind him, he spared a moment, watching *Joanna* gather the table. Her eyes lifted willingly and, turning her head, said a second time with the same musicality in voice, as if she had not abandoned for a minute the sorrows of the small island for the comforts of great *Alexandria*:

'Good morning, *Nikola*!'

The entrance to the shop formed a right angle with the exit, where the stairs led from the first floor and was located facing *Arais Street*. Turning from the alley, with his left shoulder almost touching the edge of the wall and projecting his hand with the key to the front door, he felt a presence on his right. The key almost fell out of his hand when he recognized the approaching figure with nervous strides. Decisive strides, which shook the pavement at every step, despising the weight they carried, with each foot landing very wide from the other in both horizontal and vertical directions.

He stood there as if petrified, thunderstruck with surprise, utterly helpless for any movement, with the key extended as if asking alms from the young palm trees. The staccato sound emitted by the amber beads reached his ears, creating a completely unnerving irritation and an invisible, but extremely annoying, fluttering in the chest. It was so unexpected to meet the owner of *Lido* at this place—literally in the middle of the street—that he really could not believe his ears and almost even questioned what his eyes saw!

It was not, of course, the first time *Michalis* came to the tailor's shop. By coincidence, or for other reasons, he seemed to appreciate *Nikolas'* work, going so far as to order his costumes exclusively from him. There were many times to this day that he visited him in the shop to take measures, or to bring him some expensive *English* fabric to sew it pantaloons, or a jacket that needed correction—but these visits always took place in the late afternoon hours, when the sun had long since gone out on the low horizon. The man seemed to appreciate and sympathize with *Nikolas* and the feelings could perhaps have been mutual under different circumstances.

Between them one could not find similarities, quite the contrary! *Michael* was a single-minded bachelor, a ruthless man, a brutal businessman. All night long he could sit alone behind the guichet of the *Lido* establishment, biting into an extinguished cigar, with a bottle of whiskey for company, twirling incessantly between the thick fingers of his strong palm his inseparable rosary. His passion for money was evident and the familiar way of investing he used did not leave much room for the creation of any real friendship. And the fact that until now he did not get married, combined with the behavior he showed in his relations with women—one could almost say shy, if he was not afraid that this would anger him as much as the word *"loan shark"*, because how could a man like *Michael* be shy, or, even worse, to be afraid of women?—formed the completely wrong impression of a misogynist.

Nevertheless, the owner of *Lido* was standing in front of him at this incredible hour, face expressionless and arms hanging down, legs open in the position of the last landing of the feet, body and head leaning forward like a bull in front of the red bullfighter's cloth.

'Hey *Nikolas*, good morning!'

The tone of his voice indicated clearly that he had understood the sense of surprise caused by his unexpected presence.

On the other hand, *Nikolas'* delay in answering and seeing that the confusion he caused was greater than he expected, forced him to continue.

'You didn't expect such a morning visit my dear, I get it! Surely under the light of day, and such a bright day like this eh, you would take me for someone else who looks like me! But, no, my dear friend, you are not wrong! And I, from time to time, enjoy a walk in the mornings, but I prefer the road by the sea and, lo and behold, today, for a change, I decided to walk a little more!'

Nikolas, in the meantime, managed to recover and regain his composure, saying as if to confirm it a thunderous "good morning!" and, extending his hand in a warm handshake, almost joyfully urged the visitor:

'Come on, come inside, come inside, please!'

Feigned manners did not suit his character, but this visit was perhaps the only exception. After opening the glass door, he repeated louder:

'Go in, go in! Don't stand outside!'

'It's a little cold, but don't care, I'll turn on the stove. Come on, pass in, pass in! Sorry for the clutter, but you see on Saturdays only my assistants spin. The other days they leave things as you see them now, one on top of the other, they even leave them thrown on the floor!' he said, lifting a roll of cloth underneath and, throwing it onto the wide workbench, returning to the glass door to draw the curtains, using the laces that ended in colorful tassels that hung right and left for this reason. He tried to turn on the stove but, realizing that there was no sign of fuel, he gave up, pushing a table he had for his customers between two old armchairs.

'Sit down! Do sit! The armchair is not great, but you will find that it is comfortable. Sit down, I'll make coffee! A coffee after a morning walk is a must, a must indeed!' And, seeing *Michalis* take off his jacket and sit in the armchair, he retired behind the counter to prepare the coffee.

There was indeed clutter inside the shop. On the bench, which cut the space in two, there were unfinished patterns pinned with transparent paper, scissors of various sizes, measuring tapes and a large wooden scale along with scattered chalks, pins and other small items, garnished with the roll that *Nikolas* had just deposited by picking it up from the floor. Two *Singer* foot-operated sewing machines, threaded and grotesquely clothed, stood mute, armed with skeins—black and shiny they looked like *African* cannibals. The walls were full of shelves, with tops ranging from *cashmere* and *silk* to *linen* and *felt* in every shade. A large mirror in front of the counter and the screen, with its own separate mirror, completed the picture.

There, behind the oblong bench, confusion began to overwhelm him again and at the first twist made by the amber beads of the rosary in the enclosed space, the rhythmic rattling, brought back more intensely the irritation and the same annoying fluttering in *Nikolas'* chest. The fear, slyly carried by the owner of *Lido*, seemed to come to life through the sound of the beads that diffused in the air, and were amplified as the earthquake is amplified by the shaky walls in a low-ceilinged room.

Michalis, until the coffee was made, had time to count the tops on the shelves. Nothing special dominated his mind when he was busy with this abstract process and from the whole of the shop the only thing that vaguely came to the surface, leaving everything else out, could be summed up in the concept of "dignity" as well as in the concept of "negligence". Although he never noticed details, such as that the plaster on the walls had burst creating small craters, here and there, between the shelves and the ceiling, that painting and renovating the space was more than necessary, the mere fact of lack of heating was enough to justify his dull conclusions.

So, putting the jacket back on his shoulders, he offered *Nikolas* a cigarette and, lighting his own with the same match, said:

'You have days to be seen in our neighborhood, what's going on and you're suddenly lost?' The assurance that: "nothing important is happening, that, lo and behold, a lot of work, family obligations, visits by relatives," reassured him.

'Last night was a very good night,' he began to say, slowly bringing the lit cigarette to his mouth, holding it with his fingers there, enjoying a long puff, half-closing his eyes.

'You missed not being with us! Two amazing girls from *France* turned the club upside down with their antics! You know what I mean, don't you? In the end, there was almost a fight by some hot-blooded idiots. These *Englishmen* have no brains in their heads at all. Luckily my lads quickly set the record straight! But, what am I telling you, when you come you will understand what I am saying...'

The appeal of the case made him look the other man straight in the eye. Behind the cigarette smoke hanging on the edge of *Michael's* lips, ready to fall at the first movement, he saw two flashes popping out of his expressionless eyes. Two explosive flashes, which emphatically illuminated the dense eyebrows and the wrinkles that started from the edges of the eyes and disappeared, moving away from each other to the short sideburns. There was nothing else in the cruel face that suggested the slightest emotion.

After a while he heard him ask, shaking the ashes on the ashtray, ostentatiously tapping with his outstretched finger the calcined tip several times on the glass rim:

'How are your children? What is your daughter *Mary* doing these days?'

The slightly colored tone of his voice, in the pronunciation of his eldest daughter's name, annoyed him to an incredible degree, and he studiously avoided telling him that *Mary* was about to leave the house for a while. He did not want to mention his nephew's name. He only said:

'The children are good, they are growing up and we are unfortunately getting older!'

There was something in the silence that followed that caused the scant, yet combed, hair on the shiny skin of his skull to drool, prompting him to add:

'A little more coffee *Michael*?' and without waiting for an answer, he emptied the rest of the contents from the coffee pot into the empty cup.

However, it was obvious that the owner of the *Lido* nightclub did not want another coffee since, extinguishing the cigarette in the ashtray with sharp movements, he stood up slowly, extending his hand through the jacket thrown over his shoulders.

'I'm glad you're well my dear friend!'

And straightening the jacket on his shoulders:

'I'll be waiting for you at the club soon...'

To add after a very short pause, during which the small sparks in the dilated pupils of his raven black eyes seemed to grow stronger like fire in dry grass:

'The girls are waiting for you! You know! The good old company, as well as the new!'

Not a single muscle altered the features of the dark face while they shook hands.

Nikolas, closing the glass door, turned and quickly sat down in the armchair. He extinguished his cigarette almost immediately, twisting and pressing the residue with all the force of his trembling fingers into the large glass ashtray. He was extremely worried and had his reasons for this. If he loved counting as much as the respected owner of the *Lido* night-club, he could easily count to two—just as many as the butts lying off before his eyes, smearing the crystal transparency of the glass with small stains of ash.

Three

Abdul returned to *Arais Street* a week later. It was about ten o'clock in the morning when he pulled the horse's reins, stopping it a few meters before the iron-glass door of the tailor's shop. The day was wet, with clouds multiplying in the sky following the south wind, occasionally covering the sun, making room for its rays to pass between them, forming huge moving spots of light and shadow on the flat surface of the *Alexandrian* earth. He enjoyed driving in this weather even in winter, and as he gently drew the straps his gaze caught a beam of light emerging through the clouds.

Like most Orientals, he had, from a very young age, a poetic disposition towards nature and natural phenomena, especially in extreme situations, having once said to his wife in the midst of a not insignificant earthquake—long before the earth stopped shaking under his feet: "Your voice, *Allah*, can raise the dead! We are lucky to be able to hear your voice! Your power is great! We are lucky, we are lucky!" Looking in awe into his wife's frightened eyes, as if he saw his own soul fluttering where he would find safe shelter and protection. The cool embrace of the endless sea, the air laden with the myrrh of the desert, the blessed rain, were as close to him as the people, upon whom his love and trust rested like the ends of a table on solid ground.

With his body facing the entrance, he remained seated for a few minutes in his seat, as he did not know if he had arrived earlier than expected. His mistress's instructions were clear, but her words always left an aura of mystery hanging in the air, something like an indeterminate mixture of fear and uncertainty, when she said to him, blinking constantly, as if disturbed by the silent eagerness in his feign less expressive face: "*Abdul*, you know the way to the house on *Arais Street*, isn't it so? Yes, the three-story house with the tailor's shop on the ground floor. Tomorrow, tomorrow morning *Abdul*!" So he waited on the sidewalk, hoping someone would have heard the noise the carriage made before it came to a standstill. Lately he had become too lazy, and his body responded with increasing difficulty to the dictates of his tireless soul.

But he wasn't complaining. No, he had never complained to anyone over the years—not to his wife, nor to himself, although the latter wasn't entirely true. His patrons likewise had no complaints about his services; he was absolutely sure of it. It had been twenty whole years since the winemaking business passed from father to son, and many more before that transition. Yet, he found himself nostalgic for the old days, when the freshness of new experiences touched him through the kindness of his former master. Mr. *George* had been particularly nice to him. In contrast, his second master—the "son," as he referred to him in private conversations with his wife—bore no resemblance to his father. Not at all.

He had replaced the warmth of burning coals with indifference, turning them to ashes that began to stain the icy air.

From where he sat he could not see anything inside the store, with the glass of the front door acting like a mirror sending to his eyes the annoying reflection of the cloudy sky, completely preventing any satisfaction of curiosity about what was happening inside. His first thought was to stay there until someone noticed him, but his ass ached from the constant ups and downs of the carriage and now, so still, the evil had exceeded the limits of his endurance. Blowing a reassuring whistle, so as not to frighten the horse, he leaped to the ground. He hesitantly walked towards the door where the faded inscription on the glass informed the public in *French*: *'FAIT SUR MESURE'*.

He rested his face on the glass, just below the faded sign with capital letters, sticking his palms to his temples, shading his eyes to see better. Inside, *Nikolas'* two assistants, apparently taking a break at work, were sitting in armchairs with the coffee table between them, smoking and gesticulating in a way that left *Abdul* in no doubt that they were telling stories, that they were talking about women! *Abdul* liked to hear stories with spicy content, and the two young men who helped *Nikolas* sew seem to have had an aptitude for just that.

And the cigarettes in the drawers of the store were "among the best cigarettes in the whole of *Egypt*," as *Nikolas* would tell him in his warm voice without the slightest distrust: "Gifts of happy customers, my dear! Gifts from satisfied customers... Try one... Come on, try one! Come on, here's a whole package for you my dear! Gift from the store... Come and enjoy yourself, try one, so bravo!" Delicious cigarettes, truly worthy of the spicy stories that would come back to his mind when he smoked them alone in his abode, the small room, at the edge of the garden of the large villa, watching his wife silently set the evening table.

Abdul could not discern whether the tailor was somewhere between the fabric pieces, or behind the counter, in his usual position at the cash register, and without lowering his palms from eye level he began to slam them forcefully against the glass, while observing the reactions of the young men.

The door was opened by *Omar*, who, when he saw that the demanding visitor who was hitting the glass hard was the old coachman, took the cigarette from his mouth in a theatrical motion, bowing deeply.

'*Abdul*! What a surprise, and what good fortune brought you here to make our breakfast more beautiful?' he said, the tickling sounds of *Arabic* rising from his throat to the palate, forming comical reliefs in his half-open mouth.

'Join us! Let's offer you a cigarette! *Ishmael* is here too...' he continued to talk without taking a breath and grabbing him by the hand led him inside the shop.

It was evident that there was no inconvenience because of this interruption. Accustomed to frequent breaks, the spontaneous customer disruptions, even those of complete strangers, or beggars with outstretched hands and soiled clothes, were without exception the necessary actors of a successful show. So the genuine satisfaction felt by the coachman at this cordial welcome passed like a charged wave on *Omar's* arm. Both young men were dressed in *European* style, wearing black trousers made of expensive fabric sewn by themselves, white shirts, with the only ornaments being the black bow ties, knotted high around the neck. They looked so much like each other, always dressed the same way, that one could easily confuse one with the other.

Even *Nikolas* had a tendency to confuse their names, which was more fun than distraction, and which they, apparently tired of correcting, left uncommented. Both belonging to the lower social strata, they were not entirely unrelated to the profession for which *Nikolas* approached them a few years ago. The *Greek*, with the scanty hair and the impressive mustache, seemed very friendly behind his elegant clothes and the sincerity of his voice had managed to banish with great ease any hesitation and doubt from the souls of the young *Arabs*. Their adaptation, from sewing sacks for potatoes, to the requirements of the more refined *European* way was rather quick and was largely due to their youthful enthusiasm.

Ishmael had already risen from the armchair and, hastily emptying the ashtray of cigarette butts and ashes into a tin bin, grasped *Abdul's* free hand, prompting him with successive tilts of the head:

'What a surprise? Sit! Sit down!' he said, not deciding to put the ashtray back in place. But seeing that *Abdul* was not in the mood to sit down, since, as he explained to them with characteristically eloquent movements, his back hurt and his ass likewise "from the ups and downs of the carriage," he hastily gave up. Immediately afterwards he offered him a cigarette and tea, served in a porcelain cup from the large teapot at the edge of the counter, where resting there on the floor, in a baking pan with burning coals, it remained warm all day.

'Well dear, do you know anything that is nicer than the point where it hurts you right now? Definitely not! You, as older and more experienced in these matters, should agree! Is it not so?'

A wave of wild mirth magically changed into a mere smile on *Ishmael's* face as he emphatically stressed the word "agree," revealing his bright white teeth against the sore dark background of his drawn lips.

'Well, dear?' continued *Ishmael*, seeing that the old man seemed not to understand quite what he wanted to say.

'At the farmer's market, for example, I can immediately tell out the most beautiful woman by looking only at this very spot!'

'Oh, God is great, my dear! I understood it from the moment that, no matter how well they covered it, I could see it moving...' And wanting to take the joke even further, since *Abdul's* reactions had not satisfied him so far, he proceeded as follows—bringing the momentarily derailed train back onto the tracks of its carefully charted course:

'Listen to me now carefully, my dear friend! A photographer friend took some pictures the other day that are very interesting! What do you think, would you like to take a look?'

In the eyes of the old man he saw at once that the meaning of the word "interesting" was the least that could be matched with what sprang out of the fog that covered them. His mouth had opened wide, momentarily forgetting his impaired teeth, repeating the word "interesting" in an almost mute murmur, as if he had never heard its correct pronunciation before. In this short time, *Ishmael* had already pulled through a drawer a bundle of photographs, the size of a simple *carte postal*, and slowly brought them near *Abdul's* face.

With the photographs in hand, the old man tried to focus on the subject, half closing his eyes and lowering his eyebrows, but the scant light did not help the situation at all. He began to retreat to the side of the glass door, stumbling over a small camel imitation settee, only to stop when his back touched the glass.

Resting there, he forgot himself for a while not moving a muscle. Then he turned his body so that daylight fell vertically on the papers he held between his fingers. It did not cross his mind at all that, where he was leaning, he could easily be seen by a passerby from outside. His mouth continued to blink like a fish's mouth out of water, unconsciously exposing his tongue to the tickling of his bloodshot lips, toothless gums, and palate, in an incomprehensible murmur as lines and shapes began to reveal themselves to the light.

Stuck to the glass, he did not seem to be in a hurry to see which one was more eye-catching than the other. But the thunderous voice of *Nikolas*, who had opened the front door unnoticed and had managed to bring his head to the right angle, was added to express his own admiration.

'Oh, my naughty little birds, hey, hey, let me take a look! Wow! Beautiful, huh, aren't they? Ah, huh, yes indeed!'

The voice in *Abdul's* left ear was colored only by pure curiosity and had the power to penetrate, temporarily breaking the apathy of age. *Abdul* had known *Nikolas* for many years and loved him deeply. A shy smile had suddenly blossomed on his face, merging his loose lips. Without moving his eyes from the fixed focal point a millimeter, pushing *Nikolas'* shoulder with his shoulder, he began to whisper in a low voice:

'Allah u Akbar! *Ts, ts, ts! Ts, ts, ts*! ... *'Allah u Akbar*! Huh, *Nikolas*? *Ts, ts, ts*!' continuing to alternate as slowly as possible one image after another in his palms, periodically flattening his tongue in this irritating and disgusting at the same time *'ts, ts, ts...'*

His fantasies were interrupted by the noise made by *Nikolas'* clapping:

'It's time for my little birds to work! What will I tell our customers when they come? Well, tell me please, what am I going to tell them? The best thing would be to let them see the miracle of nature that *Abdul* holds in his hands! But for how long would I fool them huh? Tell me how long I would fool them?'

Nikolas' clapping and shouting was followed by a pause, not because of the noise he was making, or because there was a fear that work would be left behind, but because the front door had opened quietly for the third time this morning. *Maria's* exotic silhouette somehow covered and completely absorbed her father's attempt to restore the usual rhythm in his shop—an effort that was literary evaporated by the "good morning" she said addressing everyone, but smiling and looking towards where *Ishmael* and *Omar* were standing.

In the confusion that shrouded the clarity of thought, *Abdul* managed to hide the provocative material in the tousles of his *djellaba* and return it clandestinely to *Ishmael*. With the same camouflaged indifference the young assistant deposited the photographs immediately afterwards in one of the many drawers on the counter. These movements, the embarrassment of the old coachman, the sideways glances of the uniformly dressed young *Egyptians*, made her feel as if she was looking again in the mirror of her room. Turning to where her father was standing, she did not have time to talk to him because the front door opened for the fourth time, cutting her phrase short.

Right next to *Maria* stood the young henchman of *Lido*, who, closing the door and turning towards the center of the room, briefly lost his voice. Under his armpit he held a parcel wrapped in paper. As soon as he found his breath, coughing two or three times—first to banish the annoying embarrassment and then the damp and loaded with cigarette smoke air from his throat—he addressed *Nikolas*:

'This parcel is sent by Mr. *Michalis*, he told me that you know what to do with it...'

Naturally, his speech was mild, he pronounced the words with a musicality like that of the *Italians*, and only the word 'Michael' was emphasized differently from the others, conveying the shadow of the owner of the *Lido* more out of habit than consciously and deliberately. To *Nikolas'* reply: "Okay dear *Manolis*, leave it to *Ishmael* and tell dear *Michael* that when it is ready I will notify him personally", he did not respond directly. *Mary's* passive presence and her sideways gaze, which caught his own defenseless, delayed him long enough for *Ishmael* to strike a deafening clap!

The young henchman acknowledged the challenge in silence and, dropping the parcel into the arms of the *Egyptian*, retreated a few steps. The next moment, politely refusing *Nikolas'* treats, drowning with difficulty the tormenting desire to bend down and kiss *Maria's* hand, he resolutely opened the door to the fresh air.

* * * * *

The rain had begun to fall unannounced, chirping on the leather cover of the transport, carrying in the air the aromas of thirsty earth. The low houses with lemon and jasmine trees in the gardens, the geraniums blooming in winter, the wild pigeons clinging to the iron railings, seemed to move as if some hand was pushing them against invisible rails. Human figures could be seen from time to time behind the opened balcony doors, stretching out their arms and looking up. Others, on the sidewalks, lifted their jackets above bowed heads and sped up their step. One or two who were lucky enough to have an umbrella opened it with some delay, perhaps wanting to cool their cheeks or make sure that the phenomenon would stop briefly.

The wild pigeons, shaking their heads to see from all sides the passing carriage, let out of their chubby breasts that lullaby: 'eighteen, eighteen, eighteen'. High up, in the hitherto quiet sky, lightning suddenly struck as if a giant palm tree had been unraveled among the thick clouds. In the prolonged and imposing boom of thunder, *Abdul* turned his head back—the shy smile mingling his loose lips, because he did not want the people he respected and loved to see that his teeth had fallen—and, still looking back, said in his broken *Greek*:

'Abdul always on time, isn't it so my dear *Mary*? *Abdul* always on time! *Awuah*! *Awuah*, always on time!' And, turning forward again, he left himself in the monotonous silence of the rain.

Four

The day moved on. His assistants left, leaving him alone behind the counter taking notes in his 'books', right next to where the large teapot was lying on the floor among the incinerated coals. There was no separate office, and the long counter was configured so that the last of its many rows of drawers housed the necessary money to facilitate transactions with customers: payment receipts, backorders and the necessary—updated to the last dot—accounts for the tax office.

The key that locked and unlocked this particular row of drawers, along with the keys to the house, was always secured in his pockets. A wooden settee with four long legs and a round base served as a seat, rotating freely, according to the position needed. The lit lamp placed a short distance from his 'books', just above the last row of drawers, cut his face in two, leaving half in the shadow. In his beautiful eyes the flame of the lamp flickered, making him appear one moment smiling and immediately the next gloomy.

Just before extinguishing his cigarette in the full ashtray at the edge of the counter, bending down to close the top drawer, a silver five pound coin fell to the floor, forcing him to stoop to find it. When he lifted it, the coin flashed briefly in his open palm as he let it slide into the leather wallet he held in his other hand. His wife used to wear a silver pendant around her neck, identical in size and shape to the coin he picked up from the floor and so painstakingly secured in his purse. That silver pendant which hung from a short silver chain, allowing it to reach up to her carefully covered chest, just below her statuesque neck. He could not remember what it depicted on its polished surface. The figure of the *Virgin Mary* maybe... Yes the figure of the *Virgin Mary* but he wasn't sure.

He had already got up from the wooden settee when, putting his wallet back in his pants pocket, he proceeded to approach the upright mirror at the other end of the room. Without looking at his reflection at all at the furniture where his customers satisfied their taste, he unbuckled his belt by loosening it at his waist. With slow movements he took off his everyday jacket, which he passed very carefully on a wooden hanger with an iron neck, then hooking it again to the horizontal rally of a support holding only his own clothes. There were two similar supports at the edges of the room for customer service as well as the demonstration of a new model, and the hands of his experienced assistants shuffled the contents several times each day.

The lifting of the lapels of the shirt followed the rough unwinding of the knot of the thin black tie. Undoing the buttons of his shirt, he felt a stream of impatience running through his fingertips. Not because he wouldn't have time, after all it was still too early, but because the buttons like the heads of the *Lernaean Hydra* sprang out one after the other without end, slipping hard through the narrow buttonholes. He had to remember to tell his assistants to make the holes a little more spacious! Tomorrow morning, before they got down to anything else, he would tell them to fix it, to fix the imperfection. He did not like clothes to have imperfections. Taking it out, at last, he threw it in a laundry basket and, forgetting it there, he picked a new one from the horizontal rail.

The feeling of contact with clean clothing on his skin calmed him, the aroma of freshly washed and freshly ironed fabric, the reversal of the process relaxed him. He liked the good outfit, and as he tightened the tie around the raised collar again, he looked at himself in the mirror for the first time. Bending forward slightly, playing with his fingers right and left tightening the knot, he lowered the collar with the other repeating the same movement. Then he allowed his gaze to reach higher, where his mustache followed the lines of his lips perfectly trimmed. This was the time he spent in front of the mirror, avoiding seeing the whole of himself out of some inexplicable fear.

The narrow streets and the wide boulevards of *Alexandria*, the low houses painted in the gray color of the desert, the small or large courtyards where jasmines hid in their green arms the railings along the entire length of the low walls, the hospitable doors and windows, leaving only the tiny flowers to break the monotony of colors, still exerted upon him something of the charm of his youth. When his gaze drifted and he discovered exotic worlds in the raunchy smells of the taverns on *Ermou Street* and in the dirty alleys of *Piraeus*, in the movements of women's figures, the warmth in the noise of the *cafés*. And the south wind that blew with an almost constant intensity all day was still blowing, making the sea come closer to the land with parallel waves of impressive height. From one splash to another there was a long interval: 'Pfaff ... Pfaff ... Pfaff!'

The water was gradually breaking along the low wall, climbing the stairs to the stone openings, washing away the foam on the surface of the ground, filling the gaps between the imposing sounds of splashes with an incessant and ominous: 'sass ... sass ... sass...' The sea frightened him at night, even though his ancestors were fearless sailors. It looked completely different to him, like the wild beast free out of its cage. But defying it, as if to confirm the authenticity of his origin, he turned his back on it and sat on a bench raising his chin, orienting his nostrils in the course of the mild wind. The smell of salt water, the sparse splashes, the long intervals that succeeded made life worth living until the end.

* * * * *

But life was worth living until the end for other reasons as well.

'What would you like to eat?' he asked him in a characteristically polite voice, bending down his imposing body, leaving on the clean tablecloth the typical list of prices and food for the day. On the plain cover, the word *'Lido'*, written in bright black ink on the white background of the paper, caught the eye of those who took it in their hands for the first time, being the only ornament on it.

Manolis, the young waiter and henchman of the *Lido* nightclub, was in a good mood to serve *Nikolas* as best he could and showed it spontaneously in the way he stood in front of him, remaining arched over as if waiting to hear some precious secret.

The establishment was almost empty of people. The elevated stage in the middle of the hall deserted, with absolutely no interest at the moment, waited patiently for the lights to come on. But it was still too early. The latest incident with some reckless *Englishmen* resulted in the abrupt termination of the *French* agent's deal with the owner of *Lido* and the hasty departure of his band. The episode would not have taken the extent and turn it did if it were not for the epicene agent himself.

It seems that a drunken *Englishman* took to the dance floor while his girls were dancing. He was given the false impression that the security men of the establishment deliberately did not intervene in time to stop the "disgrace"! So he found himself in the eye of the storm in his effort to save his girls as best he could from the hands of the crude sailor, displaying rare altruism. As a result, he became the target of the rest of the large group of sailors, who had in the meantime managed to climb the stage undisturbed.

By the time the henchmen of *Lido* took matters into their own hands, he was plagued by the appetites of the drunk men, who confused him with the dancers and would surely have ripped his shirt if he did not wear it out of his pants. The *Frenchman's* statement was delightful, with his long finger pointing to the ceiling and his colored shirt trembling over his chest like poplar leaves in a storm: 'Oh! Enough! Enough! It is not possible for such things to happen during the performance! In the ancient country of the *Nile*, in the great port of the famous *Alexandria*! Oh dear, pa, pa, pa! I tell you that such things cannot happen! Tradition does not allow it, please! Tradition does not allow it, do you hear me? Oh, that's it! Enough, gentlemen! We are leaving! No more dancing ... No more ... I tell you! ... We are leaving!'

The very next day he carried out his threats, disappointing mainly the owner of the establishment and his fanatical *English* fans.

Nikolas, ignoring the list resting between his hands, looked straight into *Manolis'* eyes. How wonderful it is to have such a lad at work, he thought, gazing passively at the young man who was standing hunched over him. Because he knew that *Manolis'* real job was not only that of a waiter, an impeccable waiter in every way. His role as the head henchman of the owner of *Lido* made him, like his boss, a little distant and difficult in his relationships with other people.

'Spaghetti without sauce!' the characteristic tone of his thunderous voice, and his eyes constantly fixed on his, did not trouble the young henchman at all.

'And, listen! Tell them to cut a salad cabbage with plenty of olive oil and lots of vinegar!'

Manolis remained in his place, since *Nikolas* was still looking at him, and seeing him grab the edge of his mustache he assumed that he had not completed the order.

'Would you like bread or something to drink with the *spaghetti*, sir?' he asked.

'Yes, do bring two or three slices of bread and a jug of chilled wine... Oh, look! Bring a bottle of vinegar with you! Girls in the kitchen never put enough! Thank you so much!'

As soon as *Nikolas'* gaze was lowered, *Manolis* straightened his body and headed to the kitchen.

The *Lido* moreover employed two *Egyptians*, a legacy of the stepfather to the current owner from the old days, who shared the role of waiter and henchman like *Manolis. Yusuf* and *Mehmet,* now in their sixties, usually appeared around ten o'clock at night, when the gathering began to thicken and needed supervision. In the kitchen, food was prepared by two women, the eldest of whom also acted as a dancer when there was nothing better in the program. While the other, affectionately named *Mabrouka,* although younger, her body weight did not allow her to expose herself under the blinding lights of the elevated stage.

There was also an orchestra composed of six *Egyptian* musicians: two violins, two drums, two clarinets and an unknown number of tambourines passed through their hands, spreading the sensual rhythms of oriental music to every corner of the great hall. The position of the musicians was at the top of the circle of the dance floor and at a much lower point than the polished boards, so as not to interfere between the audience and the dancers. And the musicians came one after another shortly after ten o'clock in the evening, sitting quietly in the six special chairs and tuning their instruments improvising for an hour or so, before the pieces of the program began to play.

The people who chose *Lido* for their entertainment were men of the port, divided into two categories. The first category included permanent customers who lived and worked near the establishment, such as *Nikolas*. In the second category were classified the non-permanent customers, sailors and peddlers or soldiers such as the group of *English* sailors who caused the last incident and forced the *French* agent to leave without excuses. The second category was the one that always prevailed when the shop happened to be very crowded, and this was for the simple reason that the touts planned by the owner of the *Lido* were aimed at the port and the crews of the ships anchored there. As a result, *Lido* was most, if not always, prey to the appetites of each clientele. A clientele whose only thing in common with the previous one was that they earned their living fighting with the same beast that breathed in the stone openings.

Nikolas, scanning the tables one by one, tried to discern someone familiar to the few people present. Two small groups of three men and as many lonely men were all seated in a way that indicated that they were probably sailors from different ships. Having apparently finished their meal, those in the two small groups were chatting quietly, holding lit cigarettes between their fingers. The loners, lost in introspection, did the same, forgetting to beat the ashes on the iron ashtrays. The fiery edges of cigarettes traced different trajectories in the dimly lit space, and everyone kept their eyes on the front door, as if waiting for some elite celebrity or some major earthquake to open it.

If the celebrity they waited to open the front door with the golden knob was really the owner of *Lido*, then they would certainly feel vindicated. Because at that time, a little earlier than usual, *Michael* appeared with his dark jacket draped over his shoulders, turning his back on them in his move to close the door, before returning immediately afterwards with the so familiar rotation around his heels, projecting his hands through the jacket, letting the beads of the rosary end up at the other end of the cord: 'Tack, tack, tack!'—greeting the people in his own way.

Freshly shaved, with his thick mustache perfectly groomed, the rest of the face charged with the same energy that burned in his black eyes, looked like a baby who had just got out of bed, ready to face with optimism what was to come. And he had actually got out of bed a short time before, in the small bedroom at the back of the nightclub. He had taken his bath—he always bathed after a good night's sleep—he had carefully shaved himself with warm water, leaving his nose for a long time in his favorite towel. There was really something childish about his delay in moving forward, about this count of people sitting at the tables with the white tablecloths and empty plates, holding lit cigarettes between their fingers, observing them as if they were inanimate objects.

The rosary had remained inert during this time, with its beads mute, testifying to the feelings of the dark man that the patrons were so few. This lasted about a minute. As soon as he recognized the figure of *Nikolas*, he proceeded with the familiar decisive steps that seemed to despise the weight they carried, looking straight ahead, letting the count sink to deeper levels. Bowing slightly before him, greeting him with a subtle lip pull in a grimace that could be interpreted as a forced smile, he pulled out the empty chair and sat down beside him.

'Did you order anything?' he asked, squeezing the beads of the rosary firmly in his palm.

The shadow of *Manolis* with the tray in his hand and the words: "ready Mr. *Nikolas*!", followed by the dull noise made by the utensils in contact with the tablecloth, as his henchman left them with swift movements one after the other, cut him short.

'Would you like me to bring you something, Mr. *Michael*?'

'A chilled glass of whiskey is enough! A chilled glass of whiskey!' he said, and, turning his body definitively towards *Nikolas*, hands resting on his knees forming two parallel circles half-hidden under the thrown jacket:

'*Bon appétit* my dear! Excuse me, but this is not a good sight of a nightclub! Look!'

'These filthy *Englishmen* are to blame for the spectacle you see! And to say that they teased the dancers. Not for God's sake! Trust me, no! That's what they had their eye on! Is it because he happened to be *French*, or because he was twisting a little more than he should, or because of the colorful shirt he wore outside his pants? I don't know! Yet it was as if he were waving a red cloth against the horns of a dozen angry bulls! I don't know if it was the beers they drank, and I can swear that while the *French* women were dancing, these filthy bulls would sit and look at them like saints. Like saints! Yes, my dear! Until one of them had the inspiration to get on the stage!' he stopped abruptly, puzzled by himself.

'If things hadn't happened like this, today the situation would be very different!' he concluded after a while, pointing his finger at the empty tables again. He wanted someone to tell his complaint, and his compatriot would understand him better than anyone else. His face was bright red, the beads of the rosary squeezed, trapped in his clenched fists. Lowering his eyes after a long time from *Nikolas'* face, he saw the glass of whiskey that *Manolis* had quietly left.

Already *Yusuf* and *Mehmet* had taken their place. The first near the entrance and the second near the kitchen door. Five of the six musicians, people with little interest in the patrons despite their undoubted abilities, had sat in the chairs at the top of the dance floor. The first notes had begun to color the icy hall and *Manolis* had managed to turn on the electric lights that illuminated the elevated dance floor and the spot where the musicians were sitting, when the front door opened, and the owner of the *Lido* counted twelve sailors entering and proceeding towards the illuminated circle. For a short time, until everyone was seated at nearby tables, the owner of the *Lido* thought that the *English* team that made the fuss a few days ago was back.

'Beer please! Waiter, bring us cold bottles of beer!' One of them began to say, bringing his palms close to his mouth to make himself heard better. And as *Manolis* set off to execute the order, his boss stopped him with a nod of his hand.

'Who are they, *Manolis*, have you seen them before?' he asked. The only wrinkles that grooved his face were those that started at the edges of the eyes and disappeared, opening like bicycle rays to the short-cut sideburns.

Manolis' answer completely reassured him, although it managed to irritate him:

'No, Mr. *Michael*! They are *English*, but they are not the ones you are afraid of, the ones we wronged last time I mean!'

Visibly annoyed, because how could the owner of the *Lido* establishment be afraid of any filthy *Englishman*, he again gave a meaningful nod to *Manolis* by showing him the kitchen and saying: 'Tell *Leilah* to get ready!'

In the kitchen, the two women, having finished their work and realizing the pause created due to the reduced clientele, were talking, jumping from one topic to another, not failing to dwell on the departure of the *French* agent and his band. Both were probably the only people working at *Lido* who were delighted with this cute *'adieu'* of the lanky man in the plush shirt. His presence meant to them, as with any other band that came for this purpose, a lot of work and endless trouble. On the last day he had kissed the women, grasping their hands and bowing his head low sometimes to one and sometimes to the other, uttering so beautifully this unique word: *'adieu!' 'adieu!'*

'Isn't it great for a man to wear his shirt out of his pantaloon? It gives him something special, brings him closer to a woman, makes him more modern. Whatever you say, I really liked it! And the way he looked at me! One time I think he peeked just as I was getting ready to go out! I'm sure I saw him peeking into the dressing room mirror, but when I turned my head to see the bird had disappeared! What strange creatures men are and how shy they are you have no idea! Most of the time, trust me, it's pure disgust, they don't even deserve to be spat on!' Nevertheless, *Leilah* had managed to like the *French* agent, perhaps because the way he treated her during his short stay in *Alexandria* made her believe that he wanted to make her a member of his band. Who would say no to a trip to *Eu-*

rope? But she was no longer young enough to move him, and her face was not as beautiful as that of the women he carried with him.

'Whatever you tell me, I will insist that it is very fashionable for a man to wear the shirt out of his pants! Ha, ha, ha! *Adieu mon serin*! Ha, ha, ha, *adieu*!' she continued her monologue looking at the edges of her shoes, the shiny black pumps, rotating them around the axes of the pointed heels as if she wanted to paint on the wooden floor the melody of the *French* words.

Mabruka, apparently tired of interrupting and constantly changing the subject, had been listening to her for a while without speaking. Her chubby arms rested on her apron, and her huge breasts went up and down slowly, like the chest of a man sleeping in the quiet of the night. Jealousy no longer tormented her as it did in the old days, when they first met. They were very young then. So she listened to her at the beginning of their long-term acquaintance, filtering the meaning of sensual sounds, passing it through the filter of this deprivation. But not now! Over time she got used to it and the feeling of jealousy turned into respect and female solidarity. The current owner and former waiter had a hand in their choice, helping his stepfather to come up with and finally decide how these girls were doing for the job he wanted them. *Mabruka* remembered the two men chatting with their backs turned and heads bowed in a meeting that would change her life, and *Leilah's*, forever.

The sudden presence of *Manolis* took *Leilah* by surprise. She liked this young man. He spoke beautifully, disarmed the other with his clear speech, and she, like a woman, found ninety-nine times out of a hundred her weapons powerless against him. He would turn his back on her at the first opportunity, like someone turns his back on a wall. 'The boss asked you to get ready...' He told her, confusing her with the smile that etched on his lips, and as he entered the small dressing room that communicated with the kitchen by a narrow corridor a few meters long, he brought the music of his voice to her ears again and again. 'Oh, the men! They don't even deserve to be spit on!' she monologued, closing the door behind her.

Her father, a *European* immigrant whose true origins no one knew, disappeared from her life very early—as did her husband several years later—leaving her completely alone to find the right way through the labyrinths of the great port. 'Ha, ha, ha, the right way! Nonsense! Nonsense, *mon serin*!' she giggled, looking once again at her bright reflection in the great mirror. The sense of the musical voice in her ears receded abruptly, only to be replaced with the same speed by the uphill climb of the work that awaited her. She had no desire to expose herself now to the sights and sounds of this other kind of music, but she had no choice. She undressed slowly, emboldened by the sideway glances she cast at selected parts of her shapely body. There were times when she was jealous of *Mabruka*. Why didn't *Allah* make her fat to escape this torment?

But that was not true. No, it wasn't true! She adored her body. She loved to look at it in the mirror, and as a matter of fact enjoyed this torment. When she was on the stage she was sure she could send everyone to hell with a wave of her hand!

Yes, to send *Lido* to hell along with all those stupid men who looked on unsuspecting. She stood up as if suddenly pushed by some invisible hand, and grasping the pencil with the red hues began to press it, pulling it onto her lips.

She didn't have a pretty face, she knew, and the colors made it rather worse—her mouth was ugly. She left the pencil next to the perfume and hairspray bottles, ignoring its fate—it almost fell to the floor—pressing her lips to spread the paint evenly. Playing with her eyelashes, she fixed the extensions, casting sideway glances until satisfied with the result, combing them upwards with a small brush. The powder formed a small cloud around her face as she applied it with a cotton stamp, hitting hard here and there, up and down. She felt better the moment she hung the large earrings in her ears. Oh, those were her favorite earrings, they looked so beautiful on her!

In the great hall the lights were dimmed and all eyes, which had previously been set on the exit door, were now oriented towards the circle of light where the elevated stage stood. Outside the light circle, in the semi-lit space, there was a commotion due to the noises made by the hands and feet of the patrons, and the voices of the *English* trying to be heard above the notes of the still disconnected music of the five musicians, who were hidden somewhere in the darkness. At that moment the bell of the front door managed to sound in the noise and disconnected notes. The commotion seemed to subside all at once, as all heads turned to see what was happening, leaving the notes to triumph on their own. A man appeared to discreetly cross the few meters separating him from the circle of light. The commotion came back and someone in the group of *Englishmen* was heard to say:

'Hey, it's that damned *Frenchman*! It's that damned *Frenchman* I tell ye!'

He had of course made a mistake since, as it turned out, occupying the sixth vacancy among the musicians' chairs, he was the musician who would tie the small orchestra—but he managed to bring the concern back to the owner of the *Lido* who immediately gave a nod to *Manolis*. This time the scattered notes also stopped and in the next moment there was absolute silence. In the middle of the light circle of the stage, *Leilah's* figure, wrapped in a gold-plated sheet, appeared as if by magic. The amber beads took the opportunity to assert: 'Tack! Tack! Tack!'

Leilah remained there, wrapped in the gold-plated sheet for some time, waiting for the musicians to start according to the suspense imposed by the program. She had her hands raised upwards, the sheet reaching to the floor, straining around her feet.

The waiting time seemed to be long for one of the *Englishmen* who, in the temporary silence, stood up and shouted derisively:

'What is this? Where is that damned *Frenchman*? He would dance better than this here scarecrow!' But he had to stop because at that moment the first chords sounded, freeing the sheet from *Leilah's* hands.

The sound of the instruments could barely be heard, and the notes seemed to come slowly, one behind the other. In this narrow window of time, until the sheet rested on her motionless feet, *Leilah* saw her audience. The next moment she turned her gaze higher, ready to lead it to hell! And she was dressed in such a way that even if she stayed still, she would probably accomplish the thing. A narrow strip of cloth, the color of gold, left the belly and legs uncovered, and higher, on the chest, another narrow strip with long fringes that reached to the belly button, completed the light garment. Her feet were completely bare, and on the fingers of her raised hands bronze bells reflected the electric lights.

Her hair, loose and black as ebony, reached down to her thin and uncovered waist. On her head there was no ornament other than her favorite earrings, and as the beat of the music grew louder, she seemed to float on its waves, while staying pinned to where the sheet was still wrapped around her bare feet. Her body pulsed with incessant ripples, just like a snake moving on the ground. The fringes vibrated gently, here and there, playing with the shiny skin of her flat belly, stroking with their colorful tassels the deep belly button. The bells on her fingertips traced curved trajectories and simultaneously rang each other as the fingers opened and closed to the rhythm of the music. At the first change of pace she stepped out of the fallen sheet and began to rotate, continuing the serpentine ripples, focusing them now on belly height.

Her legs moved so as to project as much naked flesh as possible into the light. The music continued to get faster and faster, faster and faster, carrying with it the female figure to every part of the elevated dance floor: one moment here and the next there in a dance delirium. The very air that puffed and swirled around her body reached the first seats, transporting her to where male gazes watched with evident admiration.

'By Jove! She is a goddess!'

The first exclamation of approval was followed by others.

'Never seen such a thing in my life! I wish my old man could see this! My friends, I am in paradise, yea I am I tell ye!'

'Let the damned *Frenchman* be hanged! This gal's worth the money! Oh yeah she does!'

Nikolas, from start to finish, watched the show in a bad mood. In his right hand the cigarette he was holding smoldered forgotten, swirling all the time the smoke which, pushed by the waves of air scattered by *Leilah's* dance, rose unhindered and unnoticed faded into the semi-darkness.

As soon as *Leilah* finished her dance, to the cheers and applause of the *English*, she came to the table where he was sitting, ignoring them ostentatiously.

'Why didn't you get up to dance with me, *Nikola*? You know I've been waiting for you! Why?' she said, and leaning down she kissed him passionately on the cheeks. Her gasping breath and the heavy aroma of her sweaty body, the smell of the Woman enveloped him like a balm.

Five

*A*bdul's back moved sharply as he jumped to the ground. This move revealed, apart from the caps and the fallen neck of the horse, the majestic villa of the family of 'winemakers' in all its extent. The horse had its nose a stone's throw from the tall gate, to the right and left of which stretched the whitewashed fence with the imposing black iron railings. Another carriage tied to one of the pavement poles indicated that there were likely visitors to the house.

Mary shook slightly when *Abdul's* hand touched hers. He was standing next to her, holding an open umbrella in his left hand. On his partially uncovered forehead and shaved cheeks, raindrops rolled down the white *fez*, before being absorbed further down into his straight shoulders and the wet cloth of his *djellaba*. The large garden seemed deserted, and as she walked by his side, under the protection of the umbrella, she wondered where her relatives were. The weather wasn't that bad, and she expected to meet someone on the terrace or in the decorative canopies enjoying the rain. But there was no one out there.

The front door of the villa opened with a short delay. In its outline appeared a young woman, attired in a red dress on which the white apron, caught at the waist together with straps on the back, glittered like a full moon in the night sky. Her curly hair ended in pigtails, parted in the middle, leaving a straight line visible when she bent her head. She was a tiny black girl who had an obnoxious insolence imprinted on her swollen lips.

Seeing them at the entrance, *Aimé* bowed, clearly articulating the only phrase she had been taught in *Greek*:

'Please enter!'

Inside the villa, *Aimé's* strangely sensual scent covered the smells of rain like an invisible handkerchief.

Mary was about to ask the black maid if she knew anything about the whereabouts of her cousins, when a creepy cry was heard. This was immediately followed by a bang like that of an open palm bursting with uncontrollable force on the surface of a desk. The very next moment, with a very clear articulation in *Arabic* but with all the strength one can have in one's lungs: 'Why? I am asking you! Why?' And after a very short pause: 'Why? This is preposterous! Huh! Why take the cargo from the port? Why take it? Why, the devil! I ask you why? Why, indeed!' The words came one after another, like the noise of heavy train wagons in the gaps of the iron rails. The brief outburst was replaced by a jumble of speeches. Another pause followed and a door opened, leaving at first a bright crack from top to bottom, to finish slowly and silently, just as an oyster opens its sides.

In the huge space of the empty living room, the two girls, remaining in their position, watched the door open the way one watches an accident or someone preparing to jump into the void from a great height.

At the opening, two *Egyptians* appeared dressed in *European* suits and so agitated that momentarily, crossing the living room, they passed the young women without noticing them. But a presence like *Mary's* was very difficult to disregard, even in the midst of a disaster. They both stopped their march at the same time as if they had been suddenly blocked by an invisible wall. Having removed her *raglan* jacket from her shoulders, the gray outfit she was wearing caught their attention. The two men, fists clenched, and bodies initially widely spread, as if they were about to face a common enemy, politely bowed before *Maria*, leaving *Aimé* in the dark. Then, without uttering a word, they quietly disappeared from the living room.

A sharp noise was heard in the room before the young women saw *Manolis*—son of *George Demestichas* of the 'winemakers'. His face was bright red, his hair hanging down one side, his arms open like the hands of a gunslinger before the duel, surrendered to his mental turmoil. The straight locks of his weak hair pulsed like a spider's web, and, seeing *Aimé* standing a few feet away in front of him, he said, failing to perceive *Maria's* presence:

'Please... Bring me a new glass... The other fell flat and broke... And... please... wipe the desk... The floor is full of glass!'

He sucked the air like a fish out of the water, and just as he was about to head to the large sofa against the wall, extending his left hand to rest on its back, he vaguely realized that there was another person in the room besides *Aimé*. Half-closing his eyes, he tried to identify who was standing near the black maid.

Like the *Egyptians* before him, he felt a momentary emptiness under his feet, a momentary horror at the sight of the thin waist adorned by the wide belt. The next moment, abandoning his support, he moved sharply towards *Mary*.

'*Maria*, excuse me, but it is very strange how the human mind can forget!'

'I mean that... I don't know if you understand me?... But listen and be... I had some problems with a load... But, you know, I don't want to trouble you with topics that don't interest you!' he stopped, grasping her hands.

His breath smelled of alcohol, and *Mary* barely restrained the instinctive urge to move her hands away from his. Significantly shorter he looked her in the eyes with his wet pupils facing upwards, colorless lips half open, and his large nose protruding straight through his wrinkleless forehead. But *Abdul's* deep voice came to facilitate what her instincts commanded.

'Mr. *Manolis*, I brought things up! The rain made me slow down. The horse was restless, but everything is okay! Everything is okay now! *Awuah, Awuah*! Everything is okay now!'

Mr. *Manolis* seemed not to understand the broken *Greek* of his coachman, remaining in limbo and supporting his body with difficulty on his legs, but *Maria* took the opportunity to pull her hands as politely as she could through her cousin's hands and turning to say:

'Thank you *Abdul*, you're always so kind!'

'Strange how a man's mind can forget!' thought Mr. *Manolis*, still standing next to his cousin, watching *Aimé* replace the broken glass and wipe the fragments in the dustpan. The sharp sound of the broken crystal seemed funny to him. But these idiots, his associates, had managed to get him out of his clothes! Partners, ha! What the hell were the partners good for if they couldn't figure out that the cargo was spoiled? And a small child could see that the cargo was to be thrown away! Now he had to engage himself to see what he could do. To send it back and cancel the order, since those he called his associates had signed a cart of papers. A cart of papers without bothering to open a single barrel. Not a single barrel, for God's sake! The same story was repeating itself. He was surrounded by completely incompetent people, he knew that well. He had changed all these idiots countless times before. He had sent many of them to hell, but he had not been able to find a single one truly worthy. Not one!

But he had to calm down. A movement under his feet made him think he was on the deck of a ship in rough seas. The movement persisted and so he retreated a few steps. With his arms open he let himself sit down. He had the impression that the floor suddenly gave way. His mind was in terrible confusion, he could not see clearly. The figure of *Aimé*, as she walked away with a large paper bag in one hand, the dustpan and the wicker broom in the other, seemed to him like a very pleasant joke. But he tried not to laugh. Because even a simple smile for no reason would make him look ... Really, what would make him look like a smile for no reason? The train of his weak thinking was lost for an infinitesimal fraction of time, but he managed to escape and simply bearing a smile on his lips said:

'What is your father doing *Maria*? We haven't seen him in a long time! My mother was very pleased last week visiting you...'

An experienced ear would immediately recognize the effort to control articulation, particularly in polysyllabic words—the characteristic sticking of the tongue to the palate. And *Mary* knew from the first moment she saw him that he was not well, but she did not expect this. She knew that her father's sister's son had a weakness for drinking, but what she saw happening before her eyes was beyond imagination. To his question she paid no attention, she let it fall to the floor as the crystal glass fell from his hands. She was incredibly tired of being asked the same questions lately, especially about matters concerning her father that was indirectly connected to her mother. For this reason, she agreed to leave her abode for a few days, to change her air, to change psychology. She would prefer a thousand times if he asked her in which store she last shopped, or what it was she bought there, or even better, what she would like more: a necklace or maybe a pair of earrings? So, taking advantage of his situation, she asked him her own question—about where the rest of the family might be. It did not surprise her that he had no idea, because that is exactly how he answered after a while, making a visibly great effort to understand what was being asked of him.

'I have no idea, my dear! I have not the slightest idea! Don't be surprised if I tell you that today I don't remember seeing either my wife or my daughters!'

Disappointment flooded her. She had formed in her mind a much more beautiful picture of her reception than the one she now saw unfolding before her. She looked around almost desperately. In the large living room, the light of the gray day from the large balcony doors mingled with the shadows of the furniture, creating enigmatic effects in black and white. The double curtains were drawn at the edges, bringing the garden very close, the rain continuing to fall at the same gentle pace it began. The interior was decorated, along with the furniture outside the office, by a beautiful combination of loungers: a set on each balcony door, including four-seater sofas with armchairs at each end and oblong low tables in between.

There were also, here and there, various poufs and seats in the shape of a camel or elephant. The imposing fireplace in the middle and with its funnel stuck to the north wall was off. Huge carpets with fringes at the edges did not leave a single square meter uncovered. An internal staircase, paved with a red carpet, led to the first floor where the bedrooms and other auxiliary rooms of the villa were located. The walls were decorated with impressive paintings dominated by the cloudy *Nile*, the gray desert, the deep blue of the *Alexandrian* Seaboard. At the edges of each painting the ornate lamps, with the light bulbs off at this hour, waited to get dark to replace daylight with their own light. The color of gold dominated the room.

'*Aimé*, please take my dear cousin's things and lead her to the room where she will stay!' the winemakers' successor began to speak again in a commendable but perfectly anticipated attempt to appear polite.

'I guess you know where our guest is going to stay, huh? Her room should already be ready, shouldn't it, *Ayme*?' and leaving no room for an answer, he continued with a second question.

'Do you know where my wife or daughters might be?' he said, straightening his hair with his hands and showing with a grimace that he did not believe in a positive answer.

Aimé, with an unexpected laugh that showed in greater depth the double pearls of her teeth, her immeasurable insolence hanging and pouring like a torrent from the edges of her swollen mouth, replied that she did not know where her lady was at this hour. But the room was ready and with a second burst of laughter, grabbing as much baggage as she could, she set out to carry out her mission. She was new to work, in this huge house, but she had quickly discovered that she could laugh at her master's face, especially when he had drunk a little too much. This man, he thought as she climbed the marble staircase, had two completely different faces. She preferred the latter. Like now, sitting on the couch, watching her climb the stairs, straightening his hair with his hands. His other face was scaring her! Sometimes it reminded her of the animals at the zoo. The way he looked at her reminded her, yes she made no mistake, of chimpanzees in cages. His gaze alone was able to lift the curly hairs on her skull. Hairs so curly that could break the teeth of the strongest comb easily. And as she reached the first head-step, at the turn of the stairs, and saw him still straightening his hair, she could not contain the spontaneous laughter that for the third time shook her breasts uncontrollably, her prominently fleshy lips, expelling hideously the torrent of her insolence.

Manolis Demestichas' anger dissipated in the same way that alcohol evaporates. And his anger may have subsided, but it brought to the surface the unpleasant result of the latter's reckless consumption. He had drunk this morning, in a short time, very, very much, exceeding even his own limits. But surely it would be that, towards the end, he changed the bottle. It seems that, although of the exact same brand, something was wrong with the second bottle. He would check it, he wouldn't let it pass like this. Many times in the past they had tried to trick him by passing him a thing in the pile. He had punished them all as they deserved. He would do the same now. And then he had completely forgotten that he was expecting visits. Strange how a man's mind can forget. But did he have an excuse, or did he not for everything that happened?

Those idiots, his collaborators! The damaged cargo! The papers with their signatures! Uh! The shadow of anger that nearly drowned him behind the double-leaf door quickly returned. And his glass, the beautiful crystal glass of one of his many collections, fell and broke on the floor! What a pity, for a few inches it would fall on the thick carpet escaping the breakage with the only damage being the stain that had already been made. However... But, yes, he would immediately replace it with an identical one. He would take note and order it today! *Aimé* had already brought a new cup, he saw it shine in her hands as the silver ring-bracelets shone in his cousin's splendid hands. That glass would now be placed on his desk, in place of the other. Because where else could this funny negro with the strange laughter could leave it? With this idea spinning in his clouded mind, he tried to get up from the seat he was sitting in. He failed on the first and second attempts. With the third he managed to stand with great difficulty on his feet. With uncertain steps, as if he were again on the deck of a ship in rough seas, he proceeded to close the door behind him. Turning around, he saw the new glass on the surface of his office—next to it the bottle of *French* brandy stood intact and provocative.

Six

The *café* on *Arais Street*, like all coffee shops in the world, was located on the ground floor. The three-story apartment building of which it was part was known by the number 7 and did not differ in anything else from the neighboring ones. And, practically, the *café* was attributed that number as its name: *'Number 7'*. The number '7' along with the word 'Number' adorned the top of the glass door and was repeated at various points of the exclusively glass surfaces that closed it around protecting the interior from dust, noise, or bad weather, while leaving the field of view free to those inside, turning the customers themselves into touts for those who walked outside.

The owner of the *café*, although *Egyptian*, served only *Greeks* because the latter slowly displaced the locals forcing him to adapt to their whims and habits. Dressed in the traditional *djellaba* and *fez* on his head, sometimes standing and sometimes sitting on the high wooden stool behind the counter, with his black eyes on constant alert, he looked like a huge mouse ready to devour even the crumbs left behind by the people sitting at the tables.

Nikolas, opening the glass door with the calligraphic description of *'Number 7'*, almost bounced annoyed by the sound that the little bell left floating in his ears. He looked up, but the bell's tongue had stopped touching the metal walls, surrendering to a mocking vibration like that of the sound that lingered in the stagnant and laden heavy smells air.

The sound of the bell was absorbed in the noise of the low ceilinged establishment and from two or three sides he heard his name shouted loudly.

'Nikolas!'

'Nikola, come sit down with us!'

'Nikola, eh *Nikola*, come sit down!'

To the cordial addresses, lowering his gaze, he replied by addressing everyone in the room:

'Oh yes, I should sit down, because if I don't do it quickly you will pick me up with the teaspoons!' And taking a few steps he sat down in the first free chair that was pushed in front of him.

'What happened *Nikoli*? Late night?'

The man opposite him, a painter from *Mytilene* nicknamed *'Boyas'*, ended his sentence by nailing his eyes with interest to the newcomer's red eyes. Like most, if not all, patrons of the *café* he was laid off work, resting his body until the next 'notice'. On his face, apart from the sparse hair that started high on the forehead leaving a large part of the skull uncovered, one could discern the lines of the hats and handkerchiefs that he often tied there so as not to stain it with paints and varnishes, securing that the sun would not burn him when the clouds were absent to protect him.

Nikolas wished it was just the night out, but he did not say anything to *Boya*. Looking around he clapped his hands forcefully:

'*Yusuf*! Hey, *Yusuf*! Make me a coffee, my good friend! Hot, black and without sugar!'

From the time he was young and wandered the streets of *Athens*, and the alleys of *Piraeus* where the sea hid unsuccessfully behind the whitewashed walls of low houses, the *cafés* were his refuge. There he never felt alone.

'I heard bad news from *Kasos*!'

The voice at the neighboring table had no chance of being ignored and turning his body along with the chair, silent because the word "unpleasant" was exactly what the island had generously offered him lately, he waited to hear the continuation of this unexpected line by touching the tip of his mustache with his right hand. The wooden chair creaked dangerously at the pressure on the floor, to mingle with the noise, the sounds of dice and burning coals on the stove.

'Do you remember *Manousos*, the fisherman? Well, he left a month ago to go fishing and to this day he has not returned to the island! Neither his boat nor he was anywhere all these days...'

Elias, Captain *Elias* as his friends called him after his being a captain of the small ferry boats in the port of *Alexandria*, stopped his laconic narration more out of lack of knowledge of details than out of the obvious concern he caused to his compatriot, who was still persistently twisting the tip of his mustache. He had suddenly drawn his gaze from *Nikolas'* gaze, slowly turning his head, perhaps seeking support from someone in the closed room. Emaciated, with a nautical cap on his head that hid his scanty hair, looking taller when standing because of his narrow proportions, he left himself suspended, augmenting the suspense, in the silence that followed. His mouth looked like a straight line where the lips hardly stood out like two faint parallel lines, one above and the other below, fading into the bones instead of into the sucked flesh of the skull. His faint mustache also stood out like a third line, shaved under the nose from one end to the other, as far as the barber's skill allowed.

The story was absolutely incredible. *Manousos, Nikolas* thought, constantly rubbing the tip of his mustache, is the best sailor on the island! The best fisherman in the whole *Mediterranean*! The best fisherman in the world, damn it! He could have made a bet, even now that the word "unpleasant" was buzzing in his ears like a swarm of disoriented wasps, that *Manousos* would manage to swim from *frie* to the coast of *Alexandria*, even if the distance was a few hundred nautical miles! A living legend of the island. A creature of the sea itself, who on summer nights preferred to sleep on his boat avoiding the heat and his home, bringing his wife to the verge of despair. He remembered him yes, just as one remembers the seagulls' movements in the clear blue sky before diving behind their carefree prey.

'That's not true!' someone shouted after a while, slamming the glass he was holding in his hands on the table and continuing standing:

'Why do you like to say things halfway or as you seem more likely to create doubts in the other? I expected more seriousness from you, Captain *Elias*! Your age should hold you back!'

Minas' face relaxed in the sudden pause that followed. In the pupils of his big eyes the inverted idols of the ossified form and sucked flesh swam like goldfish in the fresh water of a fishbowl. A sailor by profession, known to the people of the sea mainly for never staying in his service for more than two or, at best, three months, he unfolded his version of the story.

It was a real pleasure to hear him speak, because it was rare in his profession to read, and his sack always had a book on top of it. Many, in order to tease him, said that this was exactly the reason why he did not stay longer at work: "Hey *Mina*, why don't you take and other books in your bag when one is not enough for you?" His long elaborate phrases, mixed with strange words, the careful intonation of the syllables, the clear articulation, sometimes provoked the respect and sometimes the laughter of the listeners—who supported him now in this short speech until the last dot.

Nikolas felt a weight quickly leave his chest. The realistic approach of the truth automatically dispelled the unpleasant thoughts, sending them to rest on the calm bottom of the sea instead of *Manousos'* boat and him swimming to the shores of *Alexandria* helping him win the bet. And the truth seems to have been either a woman's affair, or an emergency repair of the boat. No one knew for sure at the moment. The *caique* was seen moored in the main port of *Rhodes*, polished and painted as always to perfection. The possibility of a woman's dress was the one *Nikolas* preferred as he bent down in front of the flame of the match offered by *Boyas* to light his ciga-rette. He knew *Manousos* well! He was able to even give up fishing in order to "hunt" as he said, instead of fish, the shapely legs of a completely unknown woman he happened to see sparkling in the sun.

'Well? How about *Manousos*? What do you think? Is he at the bottom of the sea or in the cool bosom of a *Rhodian* woman?'

Boya's face was bright red, and he could not restrain the cataract of laughter that was choking his throat. For a while he was shaken without being able to control himself.

Nikolas let him get back to normal, sucking small amounts of hot coffee, two or three times in a row, pulling his head back with each sip because it was so hot that it burned his lips and tongue. The little man would not do him the favor to stop even if he asked him to. He liked and was frustrated at the same time by the way his friend manifested his joy. It frus-trated him because as long as it lasted he was not able to com-municate with his environment, except perhaps for the sneak glances he cast left and right and which, if they happened to coincide with those of other men near him, acted as if they were all pouring oil on his mirth fire.

So now one of the patrons did not let the opportunity go to waste and shouted loudly:

'Come on, poor *Boya*! Say you're jealous, say you'd like to be in *Manousos'* shoes! Even if he was at the bottom of the sea you would envy him! Isn't that right?'

That finished him off. Having no other strength to laugh louder, he continued to hit his knees with his open palms, moving his body up and down with his head reaching low, between the legs, to rise again at right angles. A muffled groan came out of his distorted mouth, and his crimson face looked like an imprint of utter bliss, a safety valve in a cauldron ready to burst: 'Wow! Wow!' And then, trying to fill his lungs with the precious air: 'Ah! Ah!' This last combination was repeated a few times, with decreasing intensity, reminiscent of a balloon deflating freely in the air.

Nikolas, cigarette between fingers, let his gaze pass outside the glass surfaces of the *café*. The glittering day was moving forward full of promise. After yesterday's rain, the sun penetrated the clear atmosphere, reflecting the blinding light of its rays here and there—in the ponds with stagnant waters, in the cool leaves of the trees, in the windows of the dwellings that opened to welcome it. The road was busier than usual and the bicycles along with some motor-trucks disturbed with the noise of their wheels the quiet, which nevertheless still prevailed even outside the enclosed area of the *café*.

On the wide sidewalks, men and women alike, with headscarves around their heads, walked without haste, completely indifferent to passing vehicles, and the drivers, interpreting this indifference in their own way, honked their horns to get their attention smiling under the clear sky. Passing in front of the *café*, as if there were some hidden magnet behind the glass surfaces, everyone without exception would look inside until they were lost in the dividing corners on the roadsides. A little boy stood for a while and putting his hands on his temples stuck his nose in the glass. Surely curiosity about what so many men are doing gathered and sitting on the chairs with the tables all around, would have pushed him to look inside—because immediately afterwards, as if frightened by what he saw inside that strange 'aquarium', he ran away, leaving the mark of his breath on the glass.

Once, in the narrow streets of an island, another boy, stopping to look behind him, had turned his head forward many times and in exactly the same way, leaving only his breath floating at the intersections, before disappearing running between the stone walls. The clear sky, the low whitewashed houses, the beautiful chapels on the outskirts of the rough terrain, the endless sea, were the only witnesses to this temporary happiness...

The cigarette burn almost touched his fingers on the last puff. He left the cigarette in the ashtray without extinguishing it, lowering his hand very slowly. The cigarette smoke, which was still smoldering, rose upwards with small spins to get lost in the noise.

'Come on, *Nikolas*! What is happening to you, and you don't talk like you did in the good old days? Listen to me! I have told you and I will tell you again: Let go of the past! What is done you cannot undo! Many things are not up to us! Look ahead, my good man!'

Boyas, having fully recovered, saw in *Nikolas'* eyes two shadows that he did not like at all, and rummaging through the pockets of his jacket:

'See! *English* cigarettes!' he said, waving a blue box back and forth and stopping abruptly, with the index finger of his left hand pointing to fine print under a gold crown, he continued:

'Read what it writes here! Read! What? Don't you make out the letters? Is it too small for you? Well I'll read it myself! So listen: By appointment to her majesty the *Queen* of *England*!'

'Come, take one!' and ticking the box with his fingers he offered first to *Nikolas*, then to himself, lighting them in the same order, repeating pompously:

'By appointment to her majesty the *Queen* of *England*! Do you hear, good *Nikolas*?' And with the cigarette in his mouth he pointed with his finger, tapping it again on the box, the golden crown.

'These filthy pigs, the *English*! Ha, ha, ha! See what beautiful boxes they make! And isn't this golden crown amazing? Ha, ha, ha! Hey, what do you say *Nikola*? Ha, ha, ha!'

His whole countenance was bursting with hot lava, managing this time to hold back, releasing the excess energy in this giggle that faded abruptly in the many puff-poufs of his cigarette.

Nikolas looked for *Yusuf* and without clapping ordered a second coffee.

'Hey, Yusuf! One more coffee, good man, because this blessed evening deserves it!' he said and raising his hand up let the smoke make circles above his head.

He felt good among this simple people, although he always considered himself and his family a rank at least superior. Because he may have been a failure in general, but he felt very proud of his origins. His father was chief engineer on the *Suez Canal* and his grandparents were ship owners on the island long before the revolution. When his father was alive and afterwards, when he got married, there was a sparkle, a glow in his life that remained—albeit frayed—until now that he ordered his coffee at this *café* with the *'Number 7'*. The three-story house on *Arais Street*, a gift from his father at his wedding, the houses on the island: his family home and his wife's small mansion, were part of the veneer and glamour that in recent years was losing its strength faster and faster. And then how could he leave out his very, really very rich relatives? The new great edifice on the solid and historical foundations of the past. His sister had had perhaps the best wedding of all the *Greeks* in *Alexandria*. He was proud of that too. How could he not be?

By the time the only waiter was serving the second coffee, *Nikolas* had already smoked the *English* cigarette, forcing *Boya* to offer him another one in the same way. The small man from *Mytilene* felt disappointed because he waited for his friend to respond to his treat with a coffee treat, so before the young waiter could walk away:

'Hey *Samir*, bring me a coffee! Don't you see? Since the morning I have only drunk one!' Saying so, he glanced sideways at *Nikolas*, who seemed lost in his thoughts.

At that moment the doorbell rang again. This time the noise in the room, instead of absorbing the cheerful 'din, din, din', seemed to subside and fade away with it. Absolute silence prevailed in the room within a few seconds—like the silence imposed by the teacher's presence just before the beginning of a lesson. And indeed, the closing of the door followed by the familiar rotation around his heels, the childish way of absolute stillness after the abrupt rotation of the body, the obvious counting, for what else could be this leap of gaze from one man to another in the hall of the small *café*, had exactly the same effect. The owner of the *Lido* establishment stood like a teacher in front of his students. His eyes gave the impression that they could melt the iron if they stayed pinned on the metal for too long. The amber rosary hung on the fingers of his right hand idle.

In the silence that prevailed, *Yusuf's* voice, which had hardly been heard all day, was now heard like the first rooster's croaking at dawn.

'My dear *Michael*! What a pleasant surprise for our humble *café*!' Speaking in *Arabic*, since he never managed to pronounce a single *Greek* word correctly despite his daily interaction with the *Greeks*, his voice was unusually clear:

'*Samir*! Where are you, *Samir*! Do prepare the best table for our guest!'

He stopped looking impatiently for the waiter, turning his head here and there, waving his hands in the air like a puppet.

Michael, with the amber rosary suddenly waking up between the five fingers of his thick palm, contented himself with a nod and walked straight to the table where *Nikolas* was sitting.

'My dear!' he began to say, despising the presence of his companion and the other men in the small hall of the *café*—'I want to talk to you!'

Boyas, pushed by some invisible wave and sensing that staying at the same table with this unlikely man would be unwelcome, immediately got up, pushing his chair back so sharply that the latter fell to the floor with noise.

'Please sir, sit down!' he said, lifting it up, hastily dusting it off with his bare hands.

'Please sit in my chair!' and without waiting for a response, he took a step and sat down at one of the neighboring tables. The mirth was again inexplicably strengthened in his chest, like the swelling of the sea against the ribs of a boat.

There was something in the air from the moment the owner of *Lido* walked into the small *café* that caused *Nikolas* tremendous anxiety. *Boya's* servile undertaking affected him negatively, and at the first twist made by the amber beads of the rosary, the rhythmic 'tack, tack, tack' as the prelude to some terrible disaster, brought back more intensely the familiar irritation and the extremely annoying fluttering in his chest. Placing the *English* cigarette in one of the three recesses in the ashtray, he clapped with his free hands:

'*Samir*!'

He always turned to the assistant waiter when it came to ordering on behalf of another person.

'Prepare a coffee for Mr. *Michael*!'

Only a few days had passed since the last time he invaded the tailor's shop in the same unexpected way, giving him the impression of a void, a visit whose real purpose for reasons he could not have known was not manifested at the time. Even when, a few days later, at the nightclub, they sat side by side watching *Leilah's* sensual dance, he had the same impression of this disturbing emptiness, of this unfulfilled purpose. When he got up to leave, apart from *Leilah's* hand that wouldn't let his, he thought *Michael* would reach out his own to say: 'Wait a little *Nikola*, I want to talk to you!' And now, in the noise made by the beads of the rosary and the annoying flutter reflected in his chest, he felt as if the time for this revelation had finally arrived.

If the rosary could reveal the thoughts of the person holding it at that particular moment, then it would be a real puzzle as the beads suddenly stopped hitting each other and this had its explanation for the dark man. The ghost of a warm and colorful reflection from the distant past had blurred his vision. In it, he saw his mother sitting at one of the tables of the nightclub—the 'restaurant' as it was known at the time—next to his stepfather.

She wore a black dress, which must have been her favorite dress because he remembered her wearing it very often, and a red scarf was tied around her neck. Being very young, he wiped the tables and arranged the chairs in their proper place, making sure to upset as little as possible, yet watch every detail. His stepfather smiled when he heard her talk to him. And when she got up and started walking away, his stepfather would also get up following in her footsteps. He was used to seeing him follow her everywhere, always staying one or two steps behind, like the air she left around her dress. His stepfather reminded him of a tree surrendered to this almighty air. A feckless tree, whose leaves trembled in its passage and its branches bowed and perhaps even broke in its will. Sometimes he saw how his mother admired him when he did something with his hands: fixing a dripping faucet, the cracked glass of an oil lamp, or the broken pole on a broom. But he understood that he was doing it more to please her, the center of his world and his son's. It is strange how a man can give everything for a woman and his stepfather gave her everything.

The proofs were everywhere and their enumeration, even for him whose arithmetic was his favorite pastime, was very difficult. He took her every week—he had the impression that he would take her every day if it did not become boring—to shop in the most expensive stores in *Alexandria*: *'Ambassador'*, *'Ferrual'*, *'Pyramid'*, many more that he couldn't remember their names. He took her on excursions and trips, leaving him all alone: *Port Fuat*, *Helwan*, *Cairo*, and the great river of the *Nile*—all over *Egypt*. He was glad that his stepfather trusted him. But his feelings were confused then, and to this day they remained just as confused. These feelings would probably never be cleared up. That his stepfather had this relationship that a man can have with a woman was the only thing certain. But he could not touch the seabed no matter how much he stretched out his arms, being a simple swimmer in a sea that held him in her arms without revealing to him all its secrets. That she followed him so quickly after his last goodbye confused him even more!

Was it ever possible for such a beautiful woman to love a man so many years older than her? He was not sure. Then to this turn of fortune he owed his own strength today. He could not help but admit it, even though he had managed to multiply "at least ten times," according to his favorite arithmetic, the original fortune. He may not have bought a big house to live in, he may have preferred the small downtown room with the single bed and the cheap mirror above the sink where he shaved twice a day, but he had the money to buy the best house. Yes, the best house in the best district of *Alexandria*, and would do it if needed!

And now, as the ghost of that sweet memory faded away, freeing his field of vision, revealing the young waiter *Samir* wiping the tables with a damp cloth, his wonder came back as clear as a crystal ball under the sun: 'What kind of relationship could a beautiful and young woman have with a man many years older than her?' A bitter taste flooded his mouth. This would mean the permanent presence of another person next to him—in the same double bed forever and maybe, why not, a child, and to something like that he was not at all accustomed to.

The many years of single life taught him nothing about such an affair, and despite all the women who passed like shooting stars close to him, he was still as immature in family matters as the boy who just before left the print of his guileless breath on the window. With a sleight movement of his hand he lit a cigarette and, sucking in the smoke, let it hang on his lips. Behind the smoke and noise, which had returned to its usual intensity, he saw on *Nikolas'* face a mask of anguish. The *Greek* tailor looked at him as if he saw not the owner of the *Lido* but a ghost! The *English* cigarette had fallen unnoticed from the recess, leaving the ashes in the ashtray, smearing the tablecloth with a black, fiery stain on the edges of the circumference, a stain that was slowly growing. In the low-ceilinged and suffocating room full of cigarette smoke, at the short distance separating the tables, *Boya's* uncontrollable laughter sounded once again like the wave breaking unhindered at a rocky seaboard.

Seven

*M*anolis Demestichas, the proud successor of the wine-makers' business, was lying on the bed of his spacious bedroom. Next to him, his wife's warm body, covered with the white duvet that even hid her head, surrendered to a deep sleep. With her covered back turned to his face, it was as if she was thousands of miles away from him, even though he could touch her if he moved his body slightly towards her. He had climbed the stairs careful not to make noise, having cautiously closed his office door by turning off the light in the deserted living room.

Today was a very difficult day! It was very difficult because he had to spend many hours away from his favorite establishment, chasing the authorities to customs for the damaged cargo that his colleagues had mistakenly cleared through. The winery was a few miles away from this temple of safe transportation of goods, and as he climbed confidently into the carriage, holding the suitcase with the necessary papers in hand, he had urged the coachman to hurry:

'Move fast *Alfredo*! Speed up! We have spent too much time on this case! Hurry, before the bank finds out!'

The coachman, an *Italian* immigrant in his sixties, slender, with the thin mustache on his shaved face giving him something of the forgotten glamour of the *Roman* nobles, hopped without any delay in the driver's seat shouting loudly, letting the music of *Latin* be clearly heard in the quick intonation of vowels:

'Si, si senior! Subito! Subito!'...'

The people at customs knew him very well, but it seemed that things had changed.

'The tax collector is no longer the same *effendi*,' the clerks informed him in the long corridor with numerous doors.

This was not at all pleasant, given the great severity of the *Egyptian* authorities on similar issues, but old or new, he would not let it pass like this. He had resolutely opened, without even knocking, the door behind which he knew with mathematical precision what awaited him.

The tax collector sat at a small desk flooded with stacks of papers, ink cartridges and seals. Nowhere was there a chair or other seat, and the light, falling obliquely from a window high on the wall, created a fog in which the sullen face and rigid body of the customs official swam.

Things were not easy at all. He showed him the papers with the official seals of the chemical laboratory. The cargo was damaged before his people opened it, but the tax collector insisted:

'Listen my dear, there's nothing I can do! Look here!' He pointed his finger at the signatures of his associates on the cargo receipt documents.

'As you can see, your people put their signature on these papers, not me! It is impossible! Impossible!'

The direct reference to his associates brought again—fortunately controlled, this time, though he would happily clap his hand in the foreign office—the anger he felt when he heard the bad news firsthand. However, as time went on, he understood better that he could end the disagreement easily with him.

'Listen here! I am losing a lot of money from this case! Understand? Eh? I think you understand this very well! Listen here my good man, we need to send back the cargo as fast as possible! We need to return it now so that I can get a large portion of my money back!' And, saying these impatient words, he pulled out a bundle of paper pounds and ostentatiously left them on the table.

'This is a small gift, my dear sir!' he said at the end, and it seems that this was enough to open all the doors of the narrow corridor and the cargo to make its way back with the first available ship. The tax collector, having first discreetly disappeared the money into his deep pockets, stamped the certificates of the chemical laboratory, dipping his seals in ink before slamming them forcefully at the bottom of the official papers: 'Tap! tap! tap!' Simultaneously cancelling the official receipt papers in the same way, using red ink instead of black, erasing the signatures of his associates with cross red lines. Stepping outside into the fresh air, he felt as if he had unloaded a heavy burden among the piles of goods, in the open warehouses with the customs garbage.

The right step had been taken. The cancellation stamp gave him the right not to pay a single pound to the cunning merchants. Why the must now reached this miserable state, as if some unknown worm absorbed the degrees of alcohol one after another during the short journey, turning it into almost pure water, was something worth studying to find the cause. But he did not care much. Yes, he did not care at all how or why, and what really mattered was that, at last, the "prestige of the business" would remain undamaged and the money in the bank intact.

The smell of the sea, as he descended the steps of the customs office, loaded with the morning dew of the air, had brought to his dry tongue the feeling of thirst. The whole day before and at night he did not drink a drop, because he wanted to be sober in his negotiations with the wayward employees in the port, and this deprivation made him almost unable to enjoy whatever beauties there were in the harbor. He had searched the pockets of his shirt one by one, the pockets in his jacket, in his pantaloon, everywhere, returning to the pockets of his shirt, in a circular pantomime to no avail.

It was futile he knew, how could he carry with him exactly what he wanted to avoid? The countless reflections of the sun on the surface of the sea suddenly turned into glittering bottles, as he loved to watch them parade on the conveyor belts and shelves of the bottling plant. He often left his office in the winery to find himself in the area of 'manufacturing' and his favorite place was the final stage, in the bottling plant, where the sealing, the labels with the inscription of his surname on each bottle, gave him the unique sense of creation. Therein lay his great power! In these bottlenecks lay the secret of his personal wealth but at the same time of his great weakness. He had thought of taking with him a bottle of his favorite brandy, or one of the freshly sealed bottles from the shelves of the bottling plant, to give it as a gift to the tax collector. But at the last minute he changed his mind, taking the bottle out of the suitcase with the papers of receipt of the cargo and the certificates of the *Egyptian* chemical laboratory, fearing that he would not bear the temptation to part with it. Ah! one of the best brandy this *'Napoléon'*! Gift from his good friends, merchants from cosmopolitan *Paris*! He had left it in his drawer in order to bring it home when everything was fine.

His wife's steady breathing was proof that he was not dreaming—but he felt like she was thousands of miles away. For some reason he could not sleep, the ceiling seemed strangely lit as if his thoughts were projected there. Perhaps because today he bypassed the support of his peculiar alliance. He did not drink a drop today. He did not even put a drop in his mouth when he was done with the customs case, the rest of the day at the winery. He turned nervously, changing his position in bed. No, he did not put a drop in his mouth even when he came home late, and, groping again with his hands in the protective warmth of the mattress, repeating the same pantomime, he believed for a moment that he would find there the drops that would cool his deprived throat.

In vain! His nervousness grew. He could no longer lie down and shook the mattress abruptly and rose to his feet without sitting at all on the edge of the bed. In the complete darkness of the bedroom he needed no help to find the closed door. He walked out into the hallway. The distance to the edge at the beginning of the stairs seemed endless to him. In the silence of the night, his footsteps left their imprint on the rich pile of the expensive carpet, like the heavy paws of pre-historic dinosaurs on wet sand. He went down the stairs resting his hand on the handrail, stopping at every step as if he feared that he had abandoned something valuable behind him or that a bottomless abyss was opening beneath his feet. Two or three times he looked back before opening the double-leaf door of his office.

As the years went by, he felt that his wife was getting further and further away from him. 'What had changed in their lives?' he mentally wondered as he filled his glass with the brandy *'Napoléon'*, that gift from his good friends, merchants from cosmopolitan *Paris*. These people loved him truly, appreciated him for what he had accomplished so far in his life—they gave him gifts, expensive gifts, and sent him *Christmas* wish cards. Why his relatives did not appreciate him, why did they not love him just as much? He brought the crystal glass slowly to his mouth, leaving it on the tip of his nose for a while before emptying it with the characteristic shaking of the head backwards.

He filled it again, holding it with his fingertips, tilting the black bottle, enjoying the tickling sound of the glowing liquid on the glass walls, the irritating aroma in the enclosed space of the small office. But the happy conclusion of the damaged cargo case was not enough to eliminate his anger at the mishandling of his associates. Ah, those idiots of his associates had managed to infuriate him here, in this office! It was as if he was seeing these useless people again in front of him! Partners ha! What the hell were the partners who couldn't figure out that the cargo was rotted? And a small child could easily see that the cargo was to be thrown away! If he wasn't to run himself, see what he could do, send it back and cancel the order, since those he called his associates had signed a cart of papers without even bothering to open a single barrel! Not a single barrel! Yes! The same story kept repeating itself, with the risk of irreparably damaging the "prestige" of the company and himself.

Yes, yes, that was a very big truth! For who else would be harmed more by the wickedness of the world—by these opportunities presented to envious entrepreneurs in the industry, by these loathsome opportunities to the relentless pounding of competition? He was surrounded by incompetent people, he knew that well. He had changed them all countless times. He had sent many to their homes. But he had not managed to find a single one truly worthy! Not one! And he had done very well not to waste this exquisite brandy *'Napoléon'* to correct the mistake of these idiots of his 'associates'. Oh, he would get rid of them there too, among the customs rubbish along with the damaged cargo! Refilling his glass bypassed the annoying idea with the ease that one child changes the toy he holds in his hands for another.

His wife was currently lying on their bed—wrapped in warmth, in the safety of their luxurious home—of his own home! Women, huh! As long as they show no interest in how the money is made, they spend it as easily! His wife! Huh! Lately she had been turning her back on him.

'Don't push me anymore *Manolis*, please leave me alone! Leave me alone at last!' she told him more and more often in a way that disgusted him.

'Leave me alone!' the short three-word phrase resounded in his sensitive ears like a hellish echo.

What was it that was pushing her to insult him like that? Her extreme behavior had forced him to experience the hugs of other women, but this was natural, and he thought it was probably impossible to have discovered anything of this activity. Not that he cared, quite the contrary he did not care at all. In fact, there were times when it would have pleased him immeasurably to plunge his poisoned rapier into her white flesh, to hurt her irreparably with his revelations. But the cold bosoms in which he found ephemeral solace made sure that they hurt him first, as if they had conspired with his wife in a punishment worse than death itself.

Oh, he hated them! Yes, he hated them precisely for their power to punish him without mercy, without any respect for what he had achieved and the money he left in their open palms. 'What's wrong?' he asked himself, looking at the half-full glass with the glowing brandy twirling between his fingers. This was his omnipotent ally in the universe's collusion against him. Yes, his ally! His own strength, since with this he was sure that he could defeat God Himself!

The figure of a woman suddenly appeared on the back of his head. A woman without a face whose defiant gait left no room for misinterpretation of her obvious intentions. Under the transparent cloth that wrapped her, every part of her exquisite body could be seen in relief and as she climbed the stairs he had the impression that she stopped three times on the steps to make sure he was following. A pitch-black wave had lifted him from his office armchair, blinding him, frighteningly disappearing the steps beneath his feet, hiding the dangers with which he was destined to run into. He had not been drinking! No, he had not drunk more than four or five glasses. This almost full bottle of brandy *'Napoléon'* on his desk was his witness. No, he had not drunk for three days now, he was sure of it—just as he was sure that the door that he opened in the long hallway of the luxurious mansion was not the door to his bedroom.

Eight

'Well! What is going on? Will you tell me what this strange man wanted here?'

Boyas, seeing the owner of *Lido* closing the glass-door of the *café*, had returned to his seat where the smoke from the cigarette of the soft-spoken dark man was still smoldering in the ashtray. His face was still red, his lips trembling slightly, trying to contain a new torrent of laughter.

With his hands resting on his knees, his uncombed hair raised, revealing his broad forehead, he looked like an *Aristophanes* caricature. While he was at the next table, curiosity tormented him because he had never been lucky enough to see *Michalis* up close. He knew him, of course, just as almost the entire *Greek* community of *Alexandria* knew the famous owner of the *Lido* nightclub, but he belonged to that category of men who thought that it was not worth wasting a single shilling to enjoy the fun and spectacle he offered in his infamous establishment. Yes, he knew him, but only vaguely so, because although he had often shown interest in the stories of those who belonged to the other camp, he had not succumbed to temptation even once until now, thus leaving the personality of the peculiar man floating in a veil of mystery.

But *Nikolas* hardly heard a single word, much less the meaning of the dictum in the puzzled face of the small man, and although he turned his gaze it is doubtful whether he formed any clear picture of his friend in his confused mind. The seriousness of the matter wrapped excruciatingly around his neck, removing any vestiges of clarity left by the difficult night. Then again, how could it not be, since he himself had almost felt and seen it with his own eyes! As if the sudden light of lightning in the darkness of the night, the idea had formed in his mind, without necessarily wanting to admit it directly, leaving open the possibility of a wrong impression. The beginning must have been when they met him on that walk on the shore of *Alexandria*. Until then, the owner of *Lido* had never seen her up close enough for his act to have an excuse. It was obvious that he was impressed, which was particularly flattering for his *Mary*, considering his attitude towards women to this day.

But it was unexpected. He could not believe his ears when confirmation came in the temporary cessation of the amber beads between the thick fingers of his strong hands, that characteristic extension of his strong personality.

'Listen to me *Nikolas*...'

The consciously lowered voice was reminiscent of the sound of a train in a tunnel.

'I won't say much! I don't like too much talk! You know me better than anyone else. I have weighed the matter very carefully before making my decision... with great care!'

He had stopped suddenly, for a fraction of a second, allowing a subtle flickering of the eyelids, to continue dryly:

'I want your daughter to be my wife!'

And after a short pause, during which the phenomenon of a powerful earthquake could unfold:

'I have weighed the matter very carefully before making my decision... with great care! I want your daughter to be my wife!'

He emphatically repeated the exact same words, because he correctly formed the impression that *Nikolas* had not understood what he was talking about. And at that point the train might have stayed forever in the tunnel, since the owner of *Lido* abruptly stopped his speech and if the sun was not somewhere there to be reflected in the black holes of his eyes, there was the burning tip of his lit cigarette in its place.

Yes, he had foreseen it long before that revelation—in these ten or twelve simple words—but he never imagined that this terrible ghost would take shape, so quickly, believing that the sound of thunder would disappear into the sands of the *Sahara* unnoticed. His visits to the tailor's shop had increased lately, but he did not pay much attention, associating the event with the loan he had granted him at the end of the previous year. The warm exhortation to that implicit invitation with which he had tried to trap him, slowly bringing the cigarette to his mouth, holding it with his fingers there, enjoying a long puff half-closing his eyes, concluding without further expression on his arty face, suggesting the lure of beautiful but unfortunate dancers, hid precisely the meaning of these ten words. As did the flickering of the eyelids, the ease with which he threw away unwanted hesitations. Not that he had not used similar ways in the past to bring him to the nightclub more often. Certainly not, but now things were completely different. Yes, completely different! All the time, on his last visit to *Lido*, in the shadow of the girls who left so ingloriously, there was something in the inquisitive silence of the nightclub owner that gave a frightening weight to the very air he breathed. And, now that the abscess had finally broken, the blow found him unable to react, surrendered to the terrible storm of revelation.

He first met him in this same place at the nightclub many years ago, when his stepfather was still alive, doing the waiter's job. Back then the establishment functioned like a restaurant, having port people as customers as it did now. He spoke little, but he was quick-witted, very willing to serve the people who decided to push the door with the fancy name.

His story was truly unclear. He had never met his real father, and his mother seems to have been constantly behind all, creating the web at the center of which her son now stood. And if her son's life was muddled, then her own life touched and disappeared into total darkness. The two had disembarked one rainy night, last among the crowd of passengers, she with an umbrella in one hand, clutching a black briefcase in the armpit of the other. He was almost a child, hunched over the three large leather bags with all their belongings on the pier of the port, having left behind *Piraeus*—the port that had made them bitter enough that the raindrops in the foreign land resembled a cool caress on their cheeks. It seems that his mother's savings were enough to provide them with housing, since for a long time they stayed in the luxurious hotel

'*Admiral*', causing the wonder and admiration of managers and employees.

The fact that his mother was *Christian* in religion and *Greek* in origin did not prevent her from approaching his stepfather, this man among the millions of men in this vast beehive on the *African* shores of the southeastern *Mediterranean*. In the restaurant she was always among the customers, with a red scarf tied around her long neck, changing dresses with the same frequency that waiters changed soiled tablecloths. Then she would sit in random order at all the tables, making sure with incredible acting to hide her preferences—or were there no preferences? There, talking to sailors in everyone's language with the ease that bees fly from flower to flower, looking them in the eyes, touching their hands with hers, she made them not want to leave. There were many examples of men who lost their berth forgotten in the warm smile, forgotten in the warm embrace of the woman with the red scarf. She remembered the first names of everyone who was occasionally there every day and addressed them as if she had known them for years, drawing energy through their teasing and undisguised admiration.

Their enthusiasm, the lust in the corners of their eyes, the erotic passion of the moment, was the driving force behind which this woman weaved with unerring precision her almighty web. His stepfather, sitting at one of the tables at one end near the entrance with his hookah lit, dressed in *European* garb, seemed completely uninvolved in what was happening—lost in his own world, with the only sign of his presence there being his body and the thick smoke that occasionally came out of his half-open mouth. *Nikolas* had likewise felt from the first moment the defiant warmth of this woman, as he watched her walk among the patrons and finally sit at his own table. The seemingly spontaneous and unfeigned smile that curved the closed lines of her magnificent lips under the alabaster nose, made her eyes shine like twin sun:.

'*Nikolas*! My dear! How good it is for me to see you among so many strangers! Tell me, was the salad good? Do you want me to say bring you a little more wine?'

Her beauty was a sweet temptation, and no mortal could ever find the strength to resist the deceptive sirens of the divine voice—the movements of the exquisite body in the imaginary corridors between the tables and chairs of the restaurant, the seductive aroma of the air around those dresses she changed with the same frequency that waiters changed the tablecloths.

The little man opposite him was saying or trying to say something, his whole body had drawn closer, but again his voice was lost in the noise. Still the vision of the dark man with the mute rosary in his hand held him captive! Because, indeed, as long as he remained in the small hall of the *café*, the beads did not move at all to touch each other, thus expressing the seriousness of the situation in which he was to participate soon.

'The circumstances are serious... very serious!' he replied anxiously, taken aback at the direct attack of the owner of *Lido* and the manner of his statement that seemed indisputable.

'The situation is serious... very serious! Give me some time to think... Give me some time to discuss it with *Maria*...' and changing the tone of voice, regretting it immediately afterwards: 'Your proposal is a great honor for us, but... give me some time, I can't answer you now!'

He hated himself for what he had said, but if the beads were silent, crashed tightly in *Michael's* palm, it was obvious that his anemic response irritated their owner terribly! His dark-skinned face was still not furrowed, hard and expressionless, except for the fine lines that started at the edges of the eyes and disappeared into the freshly shaved temples above the willful chin, clearly showed the intensity, the terrible irritation that he felt.

'Don't care, *Michael*!' *Nikolas* addressed him, slipping dangerously into the vortex of his interlocutor's energy, disgusted now that he was soberly thinking about it.

'I will speak to *Mary*! Don't worry, I want you to rest easy! When she gets home I'll talk to her, I'll come find you in the shop, wait for me!'

And he said nothing more except when standing up, before turning his back for good, he added with his hands at a parallel angle to the rest of the body:

'Good, *Nikola*, I'll wait for you!'

As he spun their conversation in his mind, the questions arose excruciatingly: To whom would he reveal it first? What would he say to his daughter? How would he tell her? What if he didn't tell her at all? What if he didn't utter a word to anyone, if he let it go out like the sound of thunder after a storm? But no, no, that was impossible! It was impossible because he knew very well that there was no other option in this narrow one-way street. No escape! And he was afraid to predict the end, he was afraid even to rest his fingers on the freshly dug soil. Terror began to encircle his emaciated mind. There may have been times when he admired him, but he had nothing positive to attribute to the benefit of the owner of the *Lido* establishment. Quite the opposite! His dark past, the usury, the lack of education, the big age difference...

He could have unleashed all the evils of the world without satisfying what he really felt about this man. He was afraid of him, he considered him capable of anything! Even death seemed like a funny toy in the flashes, in the inscrutable depth in the black pupils of his expressionless eyes. He was afraid of him! He admired him! He hated him! Everything contributed to the storm that his words started in his soul. Was it possible, his beloved daughter in the hands of this... this... He couldn't, he didn't want to believe it, but at the same time he was afraid to even think of a way to avoid him.

He knew him very well, perhaps better than anyone else in the whole of *Alexandria*, giving exactly the importance and weight needed to this careful 'weighing', to this terrible word. No, there was no way out, at least as long as he was tied to the chariot of his economic power. But the more he studied it, the more he felt that the solution would be given by his girl! Yes, his girl would put him in his place with her behavior, let him know that he was wrong. Besides, it was known that his relations with women were not good at all. Perhaps this sensitivity would help the thunder disappear forever unnoticed in the hot sands of the *Sahara*, leaving behind only the memory of its extinguished glow. In the noise of the *café* he saw his daughter again on the pier of the harbor—gleaming like the sharp blade of an archaic sword. The defiant chin slightly turned upwards, the black hair held high with her mother's huge toque, a unique ornament in her magnificent head. And his sister had many times warned him:

'*Nikola*, don't think of leaving our girl alone on the island even for a while! You hear? Never think of leaving her alone on the island! Never! Not even for half a day! Not even for half an hour!'

And he had never left her alone in *Kasos*. But would it not have been better if he had not heard his sister's words? Would it have been a thousand times better if he had left her there, a trophy to the best young man on the island who would have won it with his sword?

The noise and the persistence of *Boya* brought him back, dispersing presently his reverie.

'But at last, my dear, will you tell us what that *loan shark* told you? Whatever it is, don't take it to heart! Let him go to hell poor man!'

His red face was so close to his own that his saliva sprinkled him generously. The word *loan shark* made him look at *Boya*, but he did not say anything. In the background, behind the counter, *Samir* wiped the freshly washed cups with a handkerchief. Next to him, sitting on a tall stool, *Yusuf*, the *café* boss, seemed to be looking with his eyes which of the customers would ask first for a drink or dessert. His upper lip was covered by a faint mustache which, protruding at its edges, gave him, assisted by his large nose and pointed face, the appearance of a giant rat.

'Okay *Nikola*, you may not want to talk, okay leave us in the dark, but at least order something! Don't you see *Yusuf*? Don't you feel sorry for him? Come on, order some hot teas, I'll buy the cigarettes!'

Nikolas, seeing the expression of the seated *Egyptian*, its contrast with the indifference of young *Samir*, suddenly surrendered to a loud laughter.

'You're right, my dear friend! Absolutely right!' he said after a while, to add at the end with his stentorian voice:

'*Yusuf*! Hey *Yusuf*! Make us two hot teas my good man! Two hot teas! One for me and one for my good friend here!'

* * * * *

Michael, leaving the *café*, did not turn to look back. The sounds of the small hall faded at the closing of the glass door, leaving the field free to the chirps of small birds and the successive 'eighteen' of the pigeons, the cool rustle of air in the leaves of the trees of *Arais Street*. It is true that lately his concerns distracted his thoughts, interfering negatively to his favorite count. Here, for example, was surprised to find that was unable to answer himself about how many idlers were spending their time sitting on the chairs around the tables in the small *café*. The fact raised a subtle smile on his pursed lips, and since this was completely out of all prediction or calculation, he began counting his steps. He began to measure the distance between the young palm trees in the square openings of the pavement. 'One, two, three,' he counted his strides. He felt a strange elation, having to do with that decision of his—taking shape in the morning as he carefully shaved with warm water to the humble sink, looking obliquely at his face in the plain rectangular mirror—to tell *Nikolas* about these tricks of the little invisible god.

It was strange, truly strange and beyond all logic. The first time his eyes saw her on the brow of the beach, very close to *Lido*, he had felt a terrible wave of jealousy for her escort. At first he did not realize that by her side was her father, one of the best and even one of his oldest customers. He was utterly unable to put into words the beauty of this strange creature, this venomous serpent that stood before him with that defiant provocation he thought he knew so well.

His mother used to take him by the hand when he was a small child—without any warning she would grab him, surprising him each time in the same way, to show him the most unlikely things: a simple vase on the table, the new mirror in the bedroom, a platter filled with *mangoes*, a common *carte-postale* with the *pyramids*. Trivial, completely insignificant things. In those moments she held him in her arms tightly. Her loose, lightly perfumed and ebony-black hair covered him like a strange wave of serene tempest. Her eyes blazed like burning coals:

'Look *Michael*! But look, isn't that amazing? Isn't that wonderful?'

And immediately afterwards, forgetting the subject altogether, he became the center of her interest and for a long time she would sit with him whispering to him in her unique voice stories that he no longer remembered—except for the tone of that wonderful voice, which he could hear crystal clear even now in the light breath of the wind in the streets of *Alexandria*, in the murmur of the waves, in the dives of seagulls in the cool waters, in the rustling of a dress on the floor or in the voice of another woman. His mother! To this day he has not been able to decipher, he has not been able to understand what it was that made her follow his stepfather, not only in life but in death as well! He was old, of another religion, with a lot of money in his chests. Surely the latter drew her to him, a perfectly reasonable assumption. But why should she leave with him, following him a few months later to the grave? Mystery! He felt betrayed whenever the thought crossed his mind.

'*Michael*, look, isn't that wonderful?' she had shown him in a sumptuous box the amber rosary that was now clasping forcefully in his palms.

Why did she leave him so early?

The winter sun played hide and seek with the sparse clouds over his uncovered head as he left *Arais Street* behind. He twisted the string with the beads, giving it a rhythmic beat, closing his fingers sharply in his palm every third rotation, trapping them there for a while: 'clap, clap, clap-chuck!' The sound of his shoes on the concrete ground resonated with his favorite count: 'one... two... three steps, the 'clap, clap, clap-chuck!' of the rosary. Yes, his mother left very early, but she was careful to leave him in the center of the protective web she thoroughly weaved for him. A web that would not only effectively protect him but help him move forward, widening the pavement under his feet, trapping defenseless insects in the slits of its invisible threads.

'I know you're going to do just fine now that we're alone, darling!' she told him, without the red scarf around her neck but with the same charming smile on her beautiful face.

But she left too early, and if her physical presence was absent, she left behind something that could be traced in, however absurd it may seem for such a character, shyness in his relations with women.

With the familiar sleight of his free hand, he brought a cigarette to his lips and lit it, stopping for a while in the leeward part of a high fence. Further, a few meters to the left, began the wide coastal avenue where the volatile currents of salty air would make it difficult for the flame of the match to succeed in its mission. Failure frightened him, any failure, no matter how insignificant! At the slightest misstep, he felt like he was breaking a precious vase, and he wanted people—even the unknown people who were currently crossing the wide promenade—to find that he had done just fine in life.

The cigarette smoke swirled in the thick hairs of his flawless mustache and disappeared behind his back as he began his confident strides, erasing the disturbing thoughts from his mind at once. In front of him the length of the brow of the shore stretched almost in a straight line, east and west, so long that it seemed to have no end. Hidden behind the low wall where the oblong marble stalls disappeared into the depth of perspective along with the openings, the stone steps could be seen leading directly to the surface of the restless sea. 'One, two, three! One, two, three! One, two, three!' he exercised his favorite count, verifying that getting from one stall to another required exactly twenty steps. The *Lido* establishment, at a distance of about half a kilometer appeared low and completely impersonal under the sunlight and the shadows that constantly changed position in the instability of the winter atmosphere.

Nine

Stretching out his left hand, he pulled the towel that hung next to the simple mirror, without lowering his gaze for a moment from the reflection of his image on the shiny surface. But this only for a while, for immediately afterwards, as soon as he touched the towel with the other hand, he closed his eyes surrendering himself to the warmth of the cotton fabric. He had bought that towel at a very good price from some *American* sailors, but that was not the dominant thought in his mind. *Nikolas* had finally made his appearance! Last night, having finished the same shaving ritual, he did not think there was any chance of meeting him after the long three-month period since their last contact at *'Number 7' café*.

Every night, just before pushing the front door of the *Lido*, he expected to see him sitting in his familiar seat, but this failed to happen. And as week after week, with the days playing a negative role in a highly torturous succession, he had begun to doubt. So he was downright shaken when he saw him sitting at the best table in the shop, with a bottle of red wine, and a lit cigarette between his fingers. He had gone straight to him, forgetting to count or look around, as if the hundred tables in the nightclub had suddenly become just one. But he had managed to see that the bottle of wine had reached halfway and that in the iron ashtray were exactly six butts, smoked to the minimum that fingers could hold, before noticing the deathlike paleness of the man opposite him.

He was so scared by the sight of the man at the other end of the table that he spontaneously drew his gaze away, hastily sweeping the clientele into the vast sala. Twice before in his life he had seen this terrible expression on people's faces: the first when his stepfather died and the second when his mother followed him. When he raised his eyes to *Nikolas'* eyes again, he had remained silent, more out of respect for what he was seeing and less because he wanted to let him speak first. His voice, when he decided to speak after a long time, was so changed that two or three times the owner of *Lido* had turned his head, sometimes aligning the right and sometimes the left ear with the mouth of the man on the opposite side of the table, fooled to such an extent as if a stranger were there.

'Forgive me my dear *Michael*... I know there is no excuse for these three months, I know you were waiting for me... I should have come much earlier... But, believe me, it wasn't up to me... I didn't want to come like this, without something positive about your proposal...'

There was a strange kind of resignation in the tone of *Nikolas'* voice, in the expression in the drawn lines on his face, in his drooping shoulders, in the movement of the hand holding the lit cigarette. But there was also something great, the signs of which could be seen in the long spaces between words, and although *Michael* hung on the meaning of those words, neither the resignation nor the grandeur that followed it went unnoticed. At the same time, he wondered: 'Why such extreme behavior towards his person, in the honest proposal he made directly that morning in the *café*?' He could find any excuse, tell him a dry no! Yes, he would have preferred to have denied it to him in the first place if he knew he was so unwanted in the family. If *Mary* did reject him, if she put him aside for someone else, or even if she put him aside like this, for no reason, without another man in her life. If that were the case then, yes, he would have preferred a thousand times not to have even made his proposal, he would have preferred to continue the lonely path he had chosen. He had power, he had a lot of money, *Nikolas* himself owed him a considerable amount, but especially in this case he did not want to be that that would play the decisive role.

Nikolas' terrible change in behavior strangely persisted, haunting the limited space of his humble abode twenty-four hours later. It was conveyed just as, if not more, unsettling, that he almost pulled down the towel to remove the unpleasant feeling, along with the warmth around his freshly shaved cheeks—but he was deterred at the last minute by the very memory of the voice and the extremely interesting meaning hidden there.

'I talked to my daughter many times...' The strange but at the same time so harmonious oscillation continued to come from everywhere, as if the field had been completely free, as if someone had wiped out the entire edifice of the nightclub from its place, leaving him exposed to the warmth of the cotton fabric under the gentle winter sky.

The same thing had happened in the great hall, when *Nikolas'* ghost pushed him firsthand to the entrance of this strange path where, as he bent down to avoid the low ceiling and stretched out his arms to the suffocating walls, it was impossible to discern anything outside the resignation and grandeur behind the silent interruptions in his speech. At first he could not make sense of what had changed in the end, because it was definitely a long time, and his words did not properly illuminate the sad situation.

'She didn't even want to listen...'. He told him, handing over the end of the tangled rope into his own hands.

'What is that are you telling me, father?' Had continued, leaving him to guess than clear up the meaning of his daughter's decision.

Yet he had not dared interrupt him even in these dark innuendos, even when it seemed like he would not have the courage to finish and finally take him out into the fresh air, where things are as simple as numbers in additions and deductions in bills. For a long time he did not come to mind, nor had he singled out anything particularly specific, confused in his attempt to correctly decipher the meaning of his alien rants. People feared him, understood it and enjoyed it, but he wished sometimes he could convince those close to him that his character was surprising even for them. He had not succeeded, mostly because he thought he would show a kind of weakness—there was nothing he hated more than that damn word—and on the other hand there was no one really close to him to guess correctly.

It was still early to leave the four walls of his humble room for his enduring destination. He had woken up well before his usual time, but at the same time he was tired of the very slowness of the routine that would balance the circumstance, when he decided to hang the cotton towel back in place.

In less than ten minutes he finished his dressing, letting his jacket balance on his square shoulders. The small room, which served the needs of the owner, did not communicate directly with the premises of the establishment.

Placed on the back of the low rectangle, it protruded like a much smaller rectangle stuck to the south side of the large one, literally invisible to prying eyes. In addition to the oblong window with its *French* shutters tightly closed day and night there was a low door, the only communication with the outside world.

From there he came out, bowing his head slightly, without locking it, without deigning to look around, despising even the stars high in the sky. In the fist of his right hand the beads of the amber rosary were crushed mutely, trapped in the pressure of the suffocatingly small space, expressing in the best way the mood of the man who walked silently—with his head bowed as if the low door he left behind had emptied him into an equally low tunnel.

It was deeply painful, as if he were scratching with his own nails a fresh wound on his body! The persistent ghost of *Nikolas'* voice mercilessly followed in his footsteps, strangely forming the walls of the narrow tunnel that forced him to keep his head bowed rather than eventually leading him out into the fresh air.

'Yes, I can assure you that... That was the positive sign I was waiting for! But I would not have come if I didn't go a little further... I would not have come if I hadn't...'

The doorbell startled him just as he was counting the last words. The piercing sound of the bell, along with the walls of the low tunnel, prevented him from seeing his young henchman who was arranging the tables in the empty hall of the establishment. He fell on him with the momentum that his nervous strides pushed him into the enclosed space.

'Mr. *Michael*! I didn't expect you so early!'

There was nothing more natural than to fall on the guard of his enterprise at this time and the encounter had as a direct result the violent removal of the suffocatingly low tunnel that kept his head bowed and as an indirect the relaxation of the pressure of his palm on the beads of the rosary, which quickly changed to the characteristic twisting, happy greeting to what he knew and loved more than anything else in this world.

After the hasty departure of the *French* agent, he had not managed to book anything good, something that would bring people back to the nightclub, and the printed papers with the relevant advertisement were limited to the services of *Leilah* and the small orchestra of six musicians. The ideas of the printer who took care, at least every month, to change the content as he saw fit in order to limit the losses due to this very weakness. At that time it was both easy and difficult for the entrepreneur to make a deal with dance groups coming from *Europe*. Easy because there was a lot of traffic, increasing the chances of something really good and difficult because in the port of *Alexandria* there were many entertainment clubs, with the only difference in the name of the illuminated sign above the main entrance. But fortunately, there was no fear that the *Lido* would ever be without proper clientele. Indeed, anyone in this profession could sleep soundly since a walk in the harbor was enough to find out. Yes, a walk in the big harbor was enough, but on condition that the wanderer observed more carefully the names on the bow or stern of the tied ships on the concrete piers.

This fact of the rotation of ships periodically in their resting place, has been known to *Michalis* almost since he first set foot in the port of *Alexandria* and certainly long before it was included in his list of favorite subjects to measure. When his back was not turned to the sea, when he walked in the mornings with his feet shaking in the familiar and angry strides that despised the weight they carried, his gaze, equally despising the vastness of the liquid element, the suffocating embrace of the heavenly umbrella, would wander impatiently between the keel and the round mouths of the ships.

Yes, his inquisitive gaze would wander to where the rusty chains, the rusty anchors or high on the three-dimensional crescent moon at the stern of the tied ships on the piers, where the names *'ATHENA' 'MONSOON' 'PEGASUS' 'PIRAEUS' 'SAINT ANDREAS' 'MARIANNINA'* were written in large, white letters. Mythical, strange names, together with common names—such as the names of ordinary women who found a place there as well as in the hearts of the shipowners. Exotic names, each with its own distinct story, lost in the morning fog, majestic, perfectly harmonized with the slow movements of the huge keels—from the moment they would appear on the clear horizon until they were tied to the iron black studs or vice versa, when they untied and lifted the anchors to slowly disappear into the restless sea. But all this magic went unnoticed by the owner of the *Lido* night-club, giving way to the calculations of his favorite count, removing the mystery of the morning fog and replacing their strange and vague story with the dry, emotionless counting of numbers: "one... two... three... four... five!'

'Listen, *Manolis*, we must do something, this situation cannot go on like this!' In his free, ostentatiously extended hand he held some of the last printed papers, identical to those scattered in the morning on the decks of ships.

"This situation cannot go on like this, you hear *Manolis*! Look! Even *Ahmed* seems to have run out of ideas! He constantly prints *Leilah's* name, changing the order of the exact same words each time!' He knew that his henchman would support him, help him find a solution, and he felt close to him as if he was clutching in his palm a revolver of extreme precision.

Showing unusual impatience, he did not sit down to listen to *Manolis'* proposal, perhaps guessing that he would never speak unless he had something positive to answer. He moved abruptly towards the walls with his body shaking at the spring vibrations of his powerful feet, turning the rest of the electricity switches, turning on all the lights around along with those hanging from the low ceiling.

'Ha! I did not hear what you said my dear friend! But I know—I know, I know you prefer silence when you have nothing in your sharp mind! Like you prefer to leave half the lights off when there is no people to occupy our tables! That's right, that's right, my dear friend! I totally agree with you that there is no reason why all the lights should be on when it's not time to turn them on...' His gaze lowered to the spelling of the last word and turned to the front door which remained closed against the light breeze of the great seaboard.

Today, like every Monday, being a public holiday for the nightclub, left room for the staff to rest and gave him the rather annoying opportunity to part, at least for a while, with his favorite box office checks. With the first 'tack, tack, tack' in the impatient spins of the rosary beads, his gaze returned, focusing higher to the eyes of his henchman. At that moment the kitchen door was opened and in the brief glow of *Manolis'* black pupils, *Michalis* saw *Leilah's* tiny mirages approaching. Without interrupting the impatient rotation of the rosary, without stirring a millimeter, he continued:

'We have to pay, my dear! Yes, we have to pay! If we do not put our hands deep in our pockets, nothing will happen! Do you hear? Nothing at all! The best dancers, the best singers, go where there is good pay! Do you understand what I mean? Besides, this is not the first time we have faced the problem, is it?'

Leilah stood next to the two men, wanting to talk to *Manolis* about some things she needed in the kitchen. She stood strained and silent waiting to be paid attention, pouring passively the warm power of the female.

'I will telegraph all our agents tomorrow, I will try to meet their representatives here... I will...' He lowered his gaze again, this time towards the defenseless presence beside him, which may not have been able to interrupt his train of thought but managed to bring the suspicion of a faint smile to his drawn lips.

'You will see how easy it is, my dear *Manolis*, to bring more people in here! I didn't like the face of this *lulu* at all! Ha, ha, ha! Yes! But luckily the world is forgiving in our profession! He is not in a position to do us the slightest damage and thanks to this here' he swirled in the air a gold *English* pound which, grabbing it before falling to the floor, he dropped it with childish naivety at the opening of *Leilah's* apron!

'You will see how many rocking *lulus* like the one who left will parade in here! You will see!'

The change in behavior of the owner of the *Lido* establishment did not go unnoticed, prolonging the silence of his henchman who was not at all used to such spills and verbiage, especially in matters involving money. It is true that he had noticed a negligence, an indifference of his boss, after the unfortunate affair with the *French* agent. A completely inexplicable reluctance to make a deal with other bands and would love to ask him about it, to help him revive the traffic in the store. He had acquaintances at the port, many acquaintances, and if these did not reach the number of acquaintances of his boss he felt that he could help and would do so with great pleasure if asked. Yes, if this lonely man, who twisted the amber rosary again between the chubby short fingers of his hand, asked him to.

And he was so close to him that the loud sound of the beads brought down a subtle irritation, an annoying shiver in his backbone. Shorter than his henchman considerably, with square proportions accentuated by the lines of his jacket, showing his shoulders protruding hugely to the right and left of the colossal neck. The complete absence of a waist made the thick legs appear as a continuation of the square torso—like a short pole capable of lifting any weight left on it, able to inspire the same fear as the one he had felt when luck brought them to meet for the first time on the vast seaboard of *Alexandria*.

And *Leilah* did notice this change in her boss's behavior, reminding her of his stepfather and the way he treated his employees—using warm words like a genuine orientalist, rewarding maids and waiters with similar moves, but never with a gold pound! Because, if she was not mistaken, the coin that was spinning just before in the air, under the lit lights of the hall and now secured at the bottom of her stained apron, was an *English* gold pound! Holding back the urge to put her hands down to confirm the truth, she too waited for the owner of *Lido* to finish his show.

It was highly unusual to meet him so early, almost three full hours before his normal time, creating the odds for the alarm bell to sound. For years, even on holidays, she never remembered an exception to the rule. He always came after eleven o'clock in the evening to sit at his literally distant table. He never spoke to anyone except perhaps a few words, counted on the fingers of one hand, to one or other of his three henchmen. A truly strange man, because how else could he describe him? Even now he seemed to despise the presence of a woman beside him, despite the compliment with the gold coin which it would have been better to have let fall on the floor, confused by the harsh sound left by the beads between his short chubby fingers.

Leilah could not explain why this warm glow did not put aside the difficulties to get what he should—and even what he shouldn't. A man of that power would change harems of women. But not him! In the years that passed, he had not changed at all, and his body movements remained in harmony with this childish count. She had heard him count myriad times, pronouncing the numbers clearly in *Arabic*: 'one, two, three!'

He was so engrossed in this foolish process that he did not notice that her nose was but a hair's breadth from his cheek. And in the past, when his stepfather was still alive and after the *Lido* passed into his hands, she had tried many times to attract the light pulses of the twin blackholes to stand on her. Oh yes, going so far as to exploit in some of them the light dress and undeniable power she exerted under the seductive notes of the oriental music. When she was in that mood in which she knew no mortal could resist her and which was confirmed every night in the applause and shouts of dozens of ecstatic customers. But she had accomplished nothing at all! Quite the opposite. The flames in the dark caverns of his eyes were extinguished as the flames of candles in the hands of *Christians* extinguish in the sudden puff of the wind.

Yes, they retreated to fade away completely on the expressionless, icy and almost wrinkles skin of his face, where the strong willful chin was a huge sculptural question mark and the radial grooves in the temples the exception. This failure resulted in a deeply negative emotion that found expression and outlet in gossip between her and other women—like her friend *Mabruka*, for example. And the comments in these conversations were not flattering at all, because at the center of this failure was a sensitive part of herself.

* * * * *

The time from the moment *Leilah* opened the kitchen door, leaving her alone, was no more than five minutes, but for *Mabruka* it was enough to make her get up and look for her in the spaciousness of the great hall. During the winter months she did not like to stay for a minute without company. So, when she saw that her only friend was late returning, she got up, carrying the weight of her obese body from the wooden bench where she sat on the wooden floorboards, to follow with mathematical precision her friend's footsteps. She opened the practical, double-leaf door without stretching out her hands, letting the momentum of her movement take her to the other side.

For many years she had been immensely amused by this way she had learned by studying the waiters whose limbs were engaged. So, left to the joy of the game and deviating a bit from the imitation of the waiters, since she always turned her head back to enjoy the seesaw of the leaves instead of looking straight ahead, she was surprised to find that her boss was two steps away. She was about to start complaining, first to *Leilah* for leaving her alone for so long and then to *Manolis* for the kitchen knife that needed grinding, but the words froze in her mouth bringing a sudden pain in the tongue as if she had accidentally bitten it.

The owner of *Lido* was really just a stone's throw away, looking like a bewildered bull. His head was slightly lowered, his nostrils dilated, his arms hung freely downwards, parallel to the inclination of his square torso. *Mabruka* looked around, quickly pulling her eyes off the dark man, looking first for *Leilah*, then for *Manolis*, downright panicked and ready to turn her back on them at the first opportunity, but she did not have time.

'Oh, *Mabruka*! I haven't seen you walk between these tables in years!'

The direct mention of her name surprised her so much that she forgot for a while her fear and the presence of her friends, next to the imposing figure of her boss. Never before, except perhaps two or three times in the distant past, had he used her first name directly. In addition, she managed to discern something in the tone of his voice, as if he understood the panic or fear he was causing her and was trying to prevent her from turning her back on him and running back to the protection of the kitchen.

'We must all help bring people back to the nightclub! You *Mabrouka* are the best cook in the whole of *Alexandria*, but we have to find a way to advertise it properly at the port!' And the unable to utter a word *Mabruka* was astonished to see her boss pull out of his pocket a gold coin, spin it in the air under the electric lights and deposit it in the slit of her huge apron.

This act was so unexpected, so out of touch with reality, that, unlike *Leilah*, she did not resist the temptation to put both hands in the depth of her apron to retrieve the gold coin.

'Ha, ha, ha! I bet you've never seen an *English* gold pound so close!'

That was true. And utterly bewildered by the unusual advance, mixed with the sounds of the amber rosary beads, the unusually prolonged reference to her person, she countered a frightened smile to *Michael's* raucous laughter. She expected help from her friends in these taunting of her boss, why how else would she characterize his behavior, but it seems that they were allied with him by remaining mute for as long as this strange monologue lasted. They refused to even help her grasp the precious object that had fallen from her trembling fingers to the floor, forcing her to bend her huge body to catch it.

In this predicament, the irritating sound of the rosary beads continued to mingle with the growl of the bull in front of the red cloth of her dress sweeping the clean floor.

'Watch out for the pound because it is the one that will bring the people back to the tables, the sailors to try the...' His voice stopped abruptly, letting the beads finish: 'Tack, tack, tack... Chuck! Tack, tack, tack... Chuck! Tack, tack, tack... Chuck!'

Mabruka slowly rose from below as if pulled by some invisible crane hanging on the ceiling, having secured the power of gold at the bottom of her apron and immediately restored the awkward smile on her closed lips, lost in the kneeling effort. Still puzzled by what was happening in the great sala and the vague sense of guilt that she was responsible for her boss leaving unfinished his sentence.

The low tunnel, which led him from the warmth of the cotton towel to the courtyard of the nightclub and the great hall with the one hundred tables and four hundred chairs, to the generous gestures without measure, had returned to the small space that communicated with the cashier's guichet. On the four walls with the posters of 'artistic' content, on the ceiling with the uncovered electric lamp, in the bright light that made the room seem even smaller. And as the quiet night proceeded with giant steps forward, he remained hunched over and motionless, his hands resting on the wooden surface of the desk, suspended in the bosom of this strange journey. The persistent ghost, suffocatingly embracing him in the closed room brought with it shadows from the past, his mother's dress, his stepfather following it, surrendering to the swirling air it left behind.

Ten

The wide sidewalk outside the *Lido* nightclub, its illuminated sign still glowing, attracting the few insects of the winter night, was otherwise deserted under a glittering full moon near the zenith of a crystal clear sky. *Nikolas*, on his way out, stumbled on the exit steps not because he was dizzy from the wine on his empty stomach but because his legs seemed unable to support him. The owner of *Lido* had done him the honor of accompanying him down the stairs, without adding any comment or a good morning, remaining mute as he had remained mute all night at their last meeting. His attitude may have worried him at the beginning of this affair, but now, as his uncertain steps pushed him back to his humble abode, that feeling had matured into a complex emotion—an emotion that hovered between resignation, anger, betrayal, resting on the filthy clutches of immeasurable disgust.

After the unpredictable and disgustingly terrifying blow of fate, the initial feeling of rage and anger, of incredible surprise, turned into a kind of resignation around which revolved, like planets around the fiery mass of a dark sun, the remnants of the terrible blast. How could he ever have imagined that someone so close to him would so abominably betray his blind trust, the very trust with which one rests on those he loves most? He did not deign for a moment to look behind him, disgusted not at the possibility of seeing the square figure of *Michael* watching him shudder in the abundant moonlight, but at his own act.

What was it that he had done? There was no relief during his testimony—his acquiescence to this crime—sitting opposite the owner of the *Lido* establishment, nor after it. The weight on his shoulders seemed to double and his weak legs showed, alarmingly frightening him, that they would not bear to make it to the end. Indeed, for the first time in his life he felt so weak as he walked away from the nightclub trying to keep his body straight in the puddles and ridges of ground, his deranged spirit prey to the moods of a malevolent force.

What was it that he had done? He stubbornly wondered, still having a little courage to support in his uncertain steps this torturous and unusually shining burden—to let it run its course, like a shooting star in the thick darkness of grief, before it too perished in the remnants of the terrible blast, the total resignation to which he had surrendered. But as he turned his back to the sea, the mirror of which was cut in two by the long silver line of the full moon's reflection, lifting his gaze up, he knew he had no choice.

It was about that time when his daughter returned, after five or six days of absence. The same moon bathed *Arais Street* in clear light, and the relief shadows of the young palm trees stood like battered soldiers lined up in line when *Abdul* began banging his clenched fists forcefully on the wooden door. The warm bed, the clean sheets and the woolen blanket, the four walls of his small bedroom, the low ceiling and the crackles on the wooden floor, the pounding heartbeats abruptly pulled his sleeping mask in the silence of the night, but aunt *Joanna* caught up with him. She opened first, recognizing the old coachman's loud voices, and that was exactly what had dominated his clouded mind, pushing aside what he had recorded in his memory, the terrible revelations that followed the end of that night—an hour or two before sunrise.

Still, as painful as it was, as much as the very mechanism of memory seemed reluctant and untrustworthy, it was impossible not to insist on fishing every now and then in the pitch-black waters and to bring out in its transparent abstention, in the merciless light, the thorny wreaths of humiliation. The old woman had acted as a shield in the *Egyptian* coachman's unfeignedly calm narrative—a shield that his daughter had bypassed by directly seeking the protection of his arms, before leaving her almost half-faint in the warmth of his beloved armchair. The familiar *djellaba* of the *Egyptian* coachman wrapped him like the mantle of an ancient messenger carrying bad news.

'I slept in that little room...' The narrative had begun like this, strangely calm through the toothless cavern of the loathsome mouth in *Arabic*, 'when I heard the girl's screams and the loud banging on the planks of the front door: *'Abdul*! *Abdul*! Open! Open quickly!' I opened the door as soon as I got out of bed: 'We have to leave now *Abdul*! Listen! Now! Right now! We have to go... have to go...' Her nightgown was torn, her arms stretched forward like a sleepwalker trying to avoid the barriers of a nightmare... While I was preparing the horse and the carriage I was looking for someone to be seen from the house, but no one was coming. I didn't know what to do! I told the girl that I had to go and fetch the key to the iron gate, to ask master *Manolis* for it... 'The master can't give you the key...' The girl kept telling me... She was telling me, 'Don't go back, please *Abdul*! Let's leave right now! Take me home... please *Abdul*...'...'

The light seemed to dim at this point as if the rickety mechanism refused to go any further, as if it wanted to protect him—like the figure of aunt *Joanna* who had caught up with him by opening the door first, holding her head high in the unexpected storm.

The old coachman had managed to take the key from the hands of master *Manolis*:

'I was very scared because the time was inopportune, but I found him walking down the stairs to the illuminated living room... I don't know what I would do if I didn't find him there... I'd have to get the key myself. Master *Manolis* told me that he was thirsty and that in his office he had opened the last bottle of that brandy *'Napoléon'* which his dear friends from *Europe* had given him as a gift: 'Come and take a sip! I have friends, very strong friends... in *Europe*... in *Paris*... Friends who really love me!' he told me before asking me what I wanted at this time in the living room. I told him that our visitor wanted to go back to her family, that he had to give me the key... He gave it to me after filling his glass, saying as he picked it up: 'Very well, but you are wrong, *Abdul*! Cheers old man! God bless the friends who care for me! Cheers to my friends...'...'

This hideous beast, his nephew, this loathsome monster claimed afterwards that he got the bedroom door wrong! His wife, as he was forced to admit in order to support the shameful 'mistake', often resisted his appetites but he moved on without paying attention, closing her mouth: 'so that the children would not hear her voices'... His palms were full of wounds trying to satisfy his sick passion...

Nikolas' clouded mind plunged like a boat in the side wave. The information he had gathered about the disaster came from everywhere—in confusing chronological order, like the forgotten mines in the dirt of a war that had ended or a war that was just beginning.

In the first steps, in the alley that led away from the sea to the interior of the great port and *Arais Street*, he stopped at the same wall that the owner of the *Lido* establishment had stopped to light a cigarette. In the murmur of the waves, in the warmth of smoke at the first puffs, the transparent shadows in the light of the glowing orbiter prevented him from proceeding on his hesitant course.

He stayed there for a while, with his left shoulder resting against the stone wall, the lit cigarette held at a minimum distance from his closed mouth. He felt very tired, his legs felt heavy like lead, unwilling to support him, and the wine no longer helped him, leaving in place of the initial euphoria a dullness and the first signs of an annoying headache pressing on with pounding beats of his wounded heart his temples—so, changing his mind, he proceeded in the opposite direction. The marble stalls on the brow of the shore were certainly much closer and in the provocative light of night it was not at all difficult to trust one's tranquility to the voices of the sirens. He chose the nearest one and sat sideways so that on his left side he could see the sea, resting one arm on the back of the bench and the other on his knee. Towards the east, at a distance of just over a kilometer, *Lido* could be easily seen among other edifices. How long would take for his daughter to become the first lady in the low building with its hundred tables, four hundred chairs and the raised dance floor, the six musicians, the three henchmen and two maids? A month, perhaps two at most!

* * * * *

The night had passed quietly. *Leilah* had danced three times—each time the clientele exceeded twenty people, *Leilah* appeared more than once on the elevated dance floor. She danced in front of a relatively small but demanding audience, consisting exclusively of *Jewish* sailors. He had come early, not because he was in a hurry to end the affair but because he wanted to catch up with *Michael,* to arrive first, to be sitting in the chair at his coffee table. The weight was such on his shoulders that he feared that his inability to carry it would betray him. It was a feeling whose inaccessible depth had annihilated him, made him so sick that even his speech seemed to disobey the weak calls of his wounded soul.

And the clear stare of the owner of the *Lido* establishment said it all, but it was obvious that he could not measure the depth of the pit through which the proof of truth—or rather the consent to its concealment—was rising. The consent to achieve through this very concealment the completion of this disgusting crime and his betrayal. Yes, it was obvious that he could not understand, confusing and misunderstanding the anguish of his interlocutor that had dared to ask for something so natural that the church rewarded with God's blessings.

And this uncertainty multiplied the hideous burden on *Nikolas'* weak shoulders. There were moments in his testimony when he was about to reveal the horrible bottom of the well, the terrible truth that tormented him but did not find the strength to do so. There he sat opposite him with his square physique strained at the elbows and his hands resting on the coffee table—clutching the amber rosary in his strong palms, the string wrapped around his short chubby fingers, the flames on the coals of his eyes lit like the lighthouse of *Alexandria* which a magic wand made appear double.

In the utter resignation he felt, under the terrifying weight of the hidden truth, he had managed at that moment to feel sorry for him. As he felt sorry for him again now that he was throwing his finished cigarette into the cool embrace of the sea, sure that it would be extinguished in the calm waves to wash up later on the shore, easy prey the next day for the garbage collectors.

In less than a minute he lit another cigarette. It was not cold, and the cool breeze seemed to emerge directly from the incessant ripples in his nostrils, without direction or orientation, along with the cigarette smoke, but the fatigue brought a sudden shiver throughout his body. From time to time small groups of men, no larger than three or at most four people, were seen at the exits of the nightclubs. Their joyful cries, their laughter, their songs in the silence of the late night, easily covered the distance to *Nikolas'* stone bench. Soon their uncertain steps would lead them to the isolation of their cells, to the lonely and cramped bunk beds of a ship or, at best, to the four walls of a small, miserable room. But he was jealous of them, he was jealous of them because they had managed to get drunk, they had managed to get what they wanted, to cross the threshold of fun.

Leilah had tried to get him started tonight, almost pulling him by the arms, when she saw that her sideways glances and meaningful head nods were not working. His reluctance had certainly seemed strange to her, and she was frightened by the sight of his face, discerning a momentary aversion to the touch of her hands to his.

And the looks of the owner of the *Lido* establishment said it all! But it was obvious that he could not measure the depth of the well above the mouth of which he was leaning in his attempt to see the bottom. Even if he pushed him in, if he threw in his face what had really happened, he would have a hard time believing it. Just as there was no doubt that sooner or later the successful entrepreneur would learn the details, maybe not exactly all, but what would change with that? Nothing! He felt utterly unable to foresee the consequences of an eventual premature revelation of the terrible secret every time he invoked the catastrophe. As if a bomb exploded again and again in his hands, leaving him dazed and half dead on the battlefield, with the only consolation—strange as that may seem—the figure of his daughter.

For she may not have spoken to him in the early days, she may have kept her head bowed when he asked her to know the details—details that her future husband might never learn—but in her gaze, which stubbornly avoided his gaze, he had quickly discerned that she had managed to absorb the terrifying blow. Even when the doctor, not the family doctor and friend but a completely unknown for obvious reasons *Egyptian* doctor who was introduced to him by one of the countless links of his acquaintances, informed them that: "My dear friends, the girl is expecting a child!"—smiling and waiting for the traditional treat of a spoon sweet after the "good news"—it was she who reacted cooler. It was a real oasis, in the inhospitable desert, the calmness with which she faced the circumstances from the beginning.

It was this oasis, this invisible triumph of his daughter—even though he did not quite understand it at this particular moment—that gave him the strength to stand with dignity against the world and the owner of the *Lido* establishment. And as he lit a third cigarette, without moving an inch from his seat on the cold stone bench, he felt the coolness of the sea air in his nostrils refreshing him, fleetingly removing the annoying headache, the depressing weight from his tired body.

Aunt *Joanna's* reaction was understandably exaggerated, but the scenes of hysteria did not help anyone, constantly challenging the tranquility of the house. At unsuspecting moments during these difficult three months, especially when it was absolutely quiet and the two children played without fighting, she would get up from her seat unannounced, letting the knitwear fall on the wooden floor, clapping her hands on her apron, muttering to herself: 'Why? Why?' And then weeping, sitting in her armchair, she would continue for a long time to murmur the same word, shaking her head incessantly right and left. Fortunately, he made sure that these sad outbursts took place when *Maria* was not with them, otherwise he would have been forced to insult her in front of her loved ones, since to his great surprise he had not managed to convince her to restrain herself.

Nikolas felt again in the silver reflections of the moonlight the shivers running down his spine. No, he did not expect this reversal of roles—of who supported whom. He considered himself weak in such matters, even if he did not dare to admit it. In the past, he had turned his back on his wife's problem. He could have helped her overcome it, but he didn't, and had it not been for the support of aunt *Joanna*, he feared that he would have completely failed in the closed and ruthless circle of family matters.

And his sister would come every other day for the first few weeks, dressed each time in a different gown, gold earrings in her ears, gold rings on her fingers, and triple rows of pearls hanging on her uncovered chest. Her curly, cotton-white hair gave the impression that were uncombed and with an air, in the imperious way in which she transferred the enormous weight of her body from one foot to the other, which testified to disbelief.

'God has punished us, my dear *Nikolas*! We must look ahead, trust the future and try to forget! It was a diabolical circumstance!' she would tell him whenever the two of them were alone in the living room, without getting any response from her brother other than the rhythmic sounds of the clock on the wall.

Maybe *Joanna* was right, but why would the good God choose to punish an innocent girl instead of those who really deserved to be punished? In his eyes there was no room for doubt. It was totally unfair to punish an innocent person in order to bring the truly guilty to their senses. And this loathsome nephew of his remained unpunished, secured in his castle, hidden behind the terrible power of money. Yet—despite the fact of being like the owner of *Lido* locked in the low tunnel of his own thoughts—he had the feeling that his sister was right about the future.

This alliance with the powerful man had its good sides. The loan, say, would stay on paper or be transformed into a donation. The *Lido* establishment would be there with its doors open, as it has been until now. However... however... How could one have fun where his daughter would take the place of a lady who was once the bait, for the hungry sailors, the tramps of the harbor? He—he would be lying if he denied it—was one of countless victims of the strange fascination of the woman with the red scarf. Yes, he would be lying if he did not admit that when he first met her, his visits to the nightclub were aimed only at her. The unpleasant thought abruptly cut short any positive elements he had begun to list for the inevitable, what he considered to be a forced alliance. This man had been very lucky in his life and free from family burdens, at the age of fifty, he suddenly decided to chart a new course.

Nevertheless, it was never uncommon for a man in maturity to choose to replace the single life with the bonds of marriage—most of the time with complete success. In *Michael's* case, however, things had entered a terribly dangerous flight before they had even begun, frightening *Nikolas*, charging him to such an extent that for the first time he felt himself so sick. What else could he do but surrender his daughter unconditionally? How different he would have felt now if he had said yes from the beginning, when in the *'Number 7' café* he was confronted with... with that proposal? How different would things have been if his beloved daughter had not listened to her aunt and had never left home? Then he would have had time to talk to her... He would have prevent the catastrophe...

At home his *Mary* had revealed it to him—although he had not realized it right away, how could he in the psychological confusion of everyone around him? She had revealed to him, without uttering a word, without looking him except fleetingly into the eyes, that the strength hidden beneath her seemingly fragile bosom would triumph in the end. The meeting with the owner of *Lido* in that café, was completely erased from his mind until the *Egyptian* doctor confirmed the nightmare that had begun to hang over the three-story edifice of *Arais Street*: 'My dear friends, the girl is expecting a child!' he had informed them with the joyful naivety of ignorance painted on his well-shaved face and his well-groomed mustache floating like a buoy in seawater—waiting after his polite bow, the spoon sweet, which, however, had been completely forgotten in the confusion of the incredible and indisputable scientific substantiation of the truth. From that moment the first thing that would come to the surface of the dirty water, in which they suddenly found themselves swimming, *Michael's* proposal was simply the most ordinary thing to happen.

'I want your daughter to be my wife! I have weighed the matter very carefully before making my decision... With great care!' he had confided to him without knowing the depth of the well over which he was bowing his head and *Nikolas* had replied, being in about the same position, that:

'I'll talk to my *Mary*, don't care at all! I want you to rest assured, when she gets home I'll talk to her... I'll come and find you in the nightclub... Wait for me!'

This very phrase of his came to the surface of the suffocating mire and from there he was caught, as one is caught by one's hair for lack of any other means. The problem with this convenient sustenance was how would he tell his wounded girl? He didn't have much breathing space, time was pressing, *Michalis* was waiting for him... But the low tunnel would help him go all the way.

The day after the confirmation by the *Egyptian* doctor, he spoke vaguely about a man who cared deeply not only about her own future but also about the future of the entire family on *Arais Street*.

'You know, my dear... There is a very serious gentleman... I mean... he asked me about you... When you were away from home, and I was waiting for you to come back to... in order to... But everything was lost from my mind after what happened...' He had stopped there, not daring to touch the steaming blood on the open wound, under the scrutiny and the huge question marks that formed in the depth of her puzzled eyes.

As he explained to the owner of *Lido*, her reaction was not at all positive at first—something that changed a few days later. This had surprised him the first time and still amazed him, here on the coastal promenade. Yes, her reaction took him by surprise when he mentioned the name of the serious gentleman behind this 'interest'. As he told her about this man, the change in her attitude was more than visible—something he did not try to hide from the person directly concerned at their meeting a few hours before in that *tête-à-tête*, with the table between their chairs and everything else: the music, *Leilah's* dance, the *Jewish* patrons, lost in some other dimension.

'When did he tell you about me, father?' she had asked him after he finished his eulogies.

The change was indeed so impressive that he had not been able to answer her directly. Was there a mutual interest, was his daughter interested in this lonely man whom *Alexandria* had welcomed when a few dozen years ago he walked down the stairs of the sip in the shadow of his beautiful mother? What else could this odious affair hide? The feeling that there might be other hidden sides was so unsettling that it briefly kept him in limbo in its delayed glow. But what did he have to fear anymore, what worse could happen to his family? In the silence of the late night, in the diminished sounds of the calm undulations, he clearly discerned the still shadows of the trees on the deserted sidewalk. The worst had passed, yes, and everyone had the right to believe that despite the difficulties, sooner or later, the walls of the low tunnel would finally make room, turning any optimism, the happy moments that the future certainly held, into a change in the life of his daughter and all those who loved her

The cigarette on his last draught burned his fingers. He threw it forcefully into the sea, using his middle finger as a small catapult, only to light another one soon after. He had lost the count and didn't know if it was the third, fourth or fifth cigarette he smoked sitting on the stone bench on the promenade.

The smoke kept him warm, the burning butt comforted him close to his whiskers, helped him see more clearly in the cold moonlight the almost embossed shadows of the trees on the square slabs of the great sidewalk, which, as if touched by the magic wand of some wandering and insignificant magician, had begun to emerge out of nowhere. In the gray halflight of the sunrise, the gaps between the square slabs had already begun to win the battle with the shadows of the trees. The smoke of his cigarette scattered a few inches from its edge, into the subtle and directionless air, to provoke him with its aroma, increasing the frequency with which his hand approached the edges of his frozen lips. The entire brow of the vast seaboard was revealed before his eyes, the outlines of tall trees replaced the fading shadows, hiding well the wandering wizard in their huge ringed trunks.

In this gray light, long before the first golden hues colored the sky to the east, the figure of a man appeared to emerge at the exit of the nightclub, where its illuminated sign still remained lit attracting the few winter insects: 'Belly dance in

Lido'. The letters of the inscription were not clearly distinguishable from the distance and the angle at which *Nikolas* stood, but *Michalis'* young henchman was clearly visible in the background of the perspective crossing vertically the promenade toward the sea. In each hand he held a large trash can, and the way he carried his body along with the burden he was carrying gave the answer to those who had the slightest doubt about the reasons why the owner of the *Lido* establishment preferred him.

A man you could trust with your eyes closed, on whom you could turn your side and sleep soundly. The man who could run the job himself, chasing the agents to organize the business properly, without asking for anything in return: 'I would like to have more opportunities to help the circumstances, I know a lot of people in the port...' He confided in him, chatting until his boss arrived, serving him the bottle of red wine and foreseeing that something very serious was bothering him. It was one of the rare times that he talked about work issues, more so with a client, but *Nikolas* had no room for misinterpretation. Despite the dire straits in which he found himself, and while the thought that such a man would be better suited to his daughter crossed his mind, he assumed that it would be unlikely that *Manolis* would know the reason for his agitation and confusion that made it difficult even to articulate correctly the measured words he managed to utter—always keeping in mind the bell above the front door. The good henchman told him about *Michael's* reluctance to book something good after the last failed attempt with the *French* dancers: *Vivi* and *Natali* and their funny escort:

'Very beautiful girls Mr. *Nikolas* and their program very good... But *Michel*...' He remembered the *French* agent's name as well as the names of the two girls, pronouncing them in his musical voice, no doubt discerning the slight flicker in the hand that had lifted the bottle of red wine to fill the empty glass. 'But *Michel* seems not to have withstood the vulgar treatment of the *English*. You should be here to enjoy the scene. What a shame to miss an otherwise good program...'

He told him about his willingness to help, noticing a change in his boss' behavior. And, while near him, he did not sit in the chair for a moment, politely declining *Nikolas'* repeated invitations to join him. He had remained there, standing and unperturbed facing him, until the moment the ringing of the bell at the entrance revealed the characteristic rotation around the heels and the black jacket passed over the shoulders, unable to hide the hands holding the amber rosary. Before leaving, he asked him, leaning a little bit towards him:

'Do you want me to bring you something besides, Mr. *Nikolas*?' But not getting the slightest answer, he disappeared quietly, obeying a nod from the nightclub owner which in the confusion of the moment went unnoticed.

He had already emptied half the bottle of the red wine and smoked half a dozen cigarettes when he sat with the confidence of the owner in the chair that his henchman had not dared to sit in. It was a very difficult moment, and it had become even more difficult because the fiery gaze of *Michael* showed that he had immediately understood that something was amiss at the bottom of the well, over which he leaned reverently as if he were going to worship or pray.

But, yes, even if he had thrown the truth point-blank in his face or pushed him to reach the mud and mire faster, he would have found it hard to believe him, thinking that his sick imagination was leading him to avoid him in a completely inelegant way. How difficult, indeed, that night was! But now he was not at all sure if he wanted to avoid him, and although his girl's future still mattered the same, he could not help but feel sorry for the man he had deliberately fooled and would fool until the end.

In the perspective of the horizon, where the sky, sea and earth merge low, giving the impression that the universe is no bigger than a child's ball, the golden disk of the sun had begun to break the blurred dividing line. Under other circumstances he would have sat down to enjoy the sunrise, but not now. On the coastal promenade, when he finally decided to get up turning his back to the light of the nearest star, the first cleaning employees had appeared with wicker brooms and huge dustbins in their hands, dragging behind them large trolleys. The place was suddenly full of seagulls, whose creepy croaks managed to frighten the naïve magician since neither he nor his magic wand could be seen anywhere. In the first steps, in the alley that led away from the sea to the interior of the great port and *Arais Street, Nikolas* stopped once again at the same wall that the owner of the *Lido* establishment had stopped to light another cigarette. Just as his future son-in-law had done, bowing reverently over the small flame of the delicate match.

Eleven

*M*ichael's young henchman could perhaps discern the wandering wizard in the colorless forms of garbage collectors dragging their carts and his magic wand to each of the wicker brooms with which they pushed the garbage into the huge dustpans. In fact, he was not far from recognizing and attributing magical properties to these people with the wicker brooms as well as to seagulls crowding low. Looking straight ahead of him, where the golden disk was emerging above the vast body of the *Mediterranean* sea like the statue of liberty, he could still see the ancient lighthouse of *Alexandria*. Indeed, the famous lighthouse as handed down by the ancient craftsmen thousands of years ago, and the master builder proudly climbing the stone stairs and lighting the hearth for the first time, which would then forever send its bright light to the decks of the ships that would approach the blessed country of the *Nile*.

One of them now seemed to slowly straighten its course, between the green and red markings on the buoys, carefully keeping the right distances, before turning to bypass the large arm of the ingress to begin the maneuvers that would bring it to tie securely to the iron studs. He was fortunate enough to hold the wooden disk of the steering wheel with his strong hands, to feel the gentle breath of the waves below deck, the enthusiasm of the crew at the approach to port. So it was not at all unreal that he could, even from so far away, hear clearly the captain's cries on the upper tier of the bridge. The wind banging with force some unfastened door on the bulwarks of the galleys, the characteristic crackling of the freshly painted boards in the tireless breath of the spirit that pushed them forward. The calm anxiety of the sailors, mixed with the anticipation of solid ground after months in the monotony of the open, without any borders and sometimes no mercy, sea. He was abandoned by his parents in its embrace, so he could not describe—if anyone was curious to ask him—what his mother looked like or if his father was as tall as he was.

This void, like the blank of an unwritten page or the blank of an unpainted picture, he took care to fill by carefully collecting patterns left and right. Touching the fragile edge of his pen with the passion of an author, the brush on his canvas full of brilliant colors, in exactly the same way that the painters of the *Renaissance* leaned over their own crates. Silently gazing at the sailors on the decks of the ships and the women wherever he could meet them. Of course, no one in the world he knew had the sensitivity to delve into the subject and those closest to him, the people of the nightclub let's say, tactfully avoided such questions since they vaguely knew his story and would not want to embarrass him.

The sailors he grew up with and the vastness of the water element managed to replace the warmth of the family, until he met the owner of the *Lido* establishment at one of the piers of the large port. There, among the oblong warehouses with the rusty irons, the wooden chests with various spare parts, the barrels of paint, the thick ropes, the rusty poles and hooks, under the hot midday sun, one could see him moving for hours—before climbing the ladder of the nearest ship, to descend again after a while from the same ladder, ready to repeat the same movements—just like the seagulls in the clear sky.

The owner of the *Lido* establishment must have watched him perform his daily duties many times against the blue background of the sea, because he knew his name and details of his story when he addressed his proposal in that unforgettable way.

'Listen *Manolis*, I want you to work with me!'

The motionless pitch-black pupils of his eyes searched deep into *Manolis* eyes as if to catch up on his answer, but it was evident that he did not have the patience to hear a word when, bent slightly forward with his arms hanging down like a bull, ready to tear to pieces the red cloth together with the toreador opposite him, he said:

'Listen here! How much do they give you? Eh? I'll give you the double!'

And when he saw him hesitate, he had continued unabated, blood flaring up on his otherwise expressionless face.

'How much do they give you? Eh? Tell me how much they give? I'll give you the triple! Do you hear me? The triples!'

He was not able then, being only nineteen years old, to understand why this well-dressed gentleman chose him among so many others, even offering him so much cash. He followed him, not for the money, but because he was really convinced that otherwise he would not get out of trouble easily if he went against his will.

The woman with the red scarf, the mother of his boss, he had not been fortunate to meet. Was his own mother like this woman? Did she look like prostitutes and paramours in dark rooms, or dancers like *Leilah*, who used their bodies to earn money? He preferred to imagine her as the simple women who did everything: cooked delicious food, washed dishes in the clear light over marble sinks where the water of the *Nile* gurgled from the opened taps, wiped every corner of the houses, made the beds with clean sheets every morning, gave birth to children. Doing everything except what he knew they do best, and he knew it firsthand. Better perhaps than anyone else, including his associates who, like him, were closer to the dark side of the moon.

But, yes, he would prefer his mother to look like the daughter of the *Greek* tailor! How strange really was this change in boss behavior, this unexpected marriage to the girl with the long black hair? The owner of the nightclub has been reluctant lately—almost a whole year—to make even one deal, to contact the various known and unknown agents. While she had appeared several times in these last six months by his side, without trying to hide, without being bothered at all by the state of her pregnancy. A second sun on bright mornings, even if the owner of the *Lido* establishment would not leave her even half a meter away from him, even if she hardly spoke while wandering here and there or sitting in chairs with elbows on the table, supporting with her hands the exquisite head.

The baby born was a boy. No one had seen it from the staff of the nightclub until today, but their boss revealed it a few days ago, opening a dozen champagnes, treating as many people as happened to push the door with the bell, having taught the waiters to say as they filled the empty glasses: "gift from the club that celebrates!" the sequel was one-word phrase yet so eloquent that the glasses were raised spontaneously in the joyful refrain: 'Let it live for you! Let your son live for you!' And *Manolis* attributed the continued inertia of his employer, the strange reluctance of those who knew him well to make a new agreement with the artistic representatives of the field, an agreement that would revive the traffic in the nightclub, to the succession of all these events.

But in a few weeks the beautiful woman with the long black hair would appear again between the tables and chairs. Yes, he found that the daughter of the *Greek* tailor was a beautiful woman, a very beautiful woman, and this woman would be constantly closer to him from now on, being the new member of their extended family. He felt in a sense very lucky for this, for this unexpected development, just as he vaguely felt that her presence there hid dangers—dangers for those who would approach the sphere of her charm.

* * * * *

Leilah, frustrated by the aspect of her large nose and mouth on her oblong face, had turned her attention to her favorite earrings. Two large bronze disks passed in the subtle holes to her soft lobes. The numerous electric lamps around the square mirror in her dressing room helped her see every detail clearly and were to some extent the cause of her frustration, despite the countless grimaces she tried to improve or, at least, come to terms with the appearance of her face. She was always hesitant to hang the earrings because she believed that this would automatically degrade the idea of the ornament and bring to the surface the weak points and especially the big nose, the misshapen jaw with teeth and lips protruding like a disproportionately large balcony in a low house. She let her hands fall down, lowering her tired gaze from the exhausting glow of the mirror. There was no longer any interest in the vicious hostile gloss of its surface. In addition, she felt so tired that if she left herself in this position she would fall asleep before she could count to three. But as she got up, she thought everybody must have left the nightclub by now.

She had been forgotten by everyone, how many minutes or how many hours it was impossible to calculate, alone in the small room. The boss, after his recent marriage, left unexpectedly early, leaving *Manolis* in charge. It was for her, as for everyone who knew him, something completely unusual. But especially for *Leilah* it was a completely unlikely occurrence, one that transcended even her most extreme, her most daring fantasies, her darkest nightmares! 'Oh, the men! Men! They don't even deserve to be spit on!' she monologued, as her hand touched the doorknob that led to the narrow corridor and the large hall of the nightclub. How could his latest achievement be understood? Really, how could anyone justify this... *Leilah* made no effort to contain the wild laughter that poured like a torrent through her breasts, shaking her entire body and the walls of the great hall from one end to the other: 'Ha-ha-ha, ha-ha-ha, ha-ha-ha!' That damned misogynist!

The man who not only showed with his incomprehensible behavior that he hated women but went further, putting aside even the direct challenges and provocations that no real man would have the strength to resist! 'Ha-ha-ha, ha-ha-ha, ha-ha-ha!' Her hysterical laughter, unrestrained in the empty hall, grew louder and multiplied in the echo, as if accompanied by thousands of other mouths together as ugly as hers, making the great hall look like a cave where some sleeping spirit suddenly awoke frightened, ready to take revenge: 'Ha-ha-ha, ha-ha-ha, ha-ha-ha!' *Leilah's* outburst was so great that she stood for a while, unable to continue her steps, resting her fingertips on one of the coffee tables.

Really, how could his latest achievement be understood? The laughter in her open mouth dried up as abruptly as it began, leaving in its place a gasping breath and a quick up and down of her chest, and the endearing epithet with which she used to mentally address him once again surfaced: 'The idiot!' Her power over men was a given, she had felt it today as much as any other night. In the first notes, when the music started and she stood motionless behind the semitransparent cloth, she knew that they were at her mercy. 'Oh, the fools!' The grudges she felt for all those down there shot like poisonous arrows every time the golden cloth fell on the boards of the dance floor, leaving her naked to the rhythm of oriental music. They could not then distinguish the big nose, her black eyes, her ugly mouth, despite the blinding light in which she swam. She brought her hand unconsciously to the lowest of her face. The sparse fluff on her chin and cheeks reminded her that she had forgotten to do *halawa*. Lately she has been neglecting herself a lot, and that was not a good sign.

And men, ha, men! They don't even deserve to be spit on! One is worse than the other! Apart from... apart from a few exceptions—like, say, that handsome *Frenchman* in the colorful shirt peeking behind the half-drawn curtain of the little dressing room. Yes, yes, fortunately there were exceptions! And *Manolis*? Ah, sweet *Manolis*! *Manolis* would be hanging around somewhere out there... He always left last, he wouldn't leave her alone... Besides, he was now the one who locked the doors of the *Lido* establishment. For the first time, while she was in the great sala of the nightclub, she let her gaze wander on the walls adorned with heavy red curtains.

Half of the lights were off, and the other half were still on, next to the large paintings with the gold-plated frames, but the young henchman was nowhere to be seen. Yes, the lights of the elevated stage were indeed off, as were half the lights of the deserted hall. "The boss left early," *Mabruka* told her, before she too left for home, but she didn't need someone to assure her of something that had become the norm so unexpectedly and against all logic, even her own logic! If there were anyone else in his place she would find a thousand and two explanations, but a man like *Michael*! Brr, she shuddered at the intense contrast of her emotions...

* * * * *

The bell at the front door mingled with the calls of the seagulls to which everyone at that moment would give a little of their time, but not *Leilah*. For her, *Manolis'* square back and the smell of the cigarette hanging on his lips were the only things that deserved her attention. There were times when the boss's henchman forgot the ugliness of her face. There were times when he longed for her as a man craves a woman and putting aside any scruples and difficulties he reached to the end, he reached the spring where the immortal water flowed—and as he took the first steps towards her, she sensed that she was guessing right. She stood beside him without uttering a word, looking at him obliquely as she had looked at herself in the mirror of her dressing room.

'You have forgotten to put on your coat, let me bring it for you' she heard him say, completely motionless and with the only witness confirming the speech being the pulsating cigarette at the edges of his shapely lips. The next second he disappeared from her side in search of the forgotten coat.

'What fools men are!' she thought as the fluttering of seagulls on their steep ditches suddenly brought the morning coolness to roll from one end of her backbone to the other. Someone from the audience today tried to get to the dance floor. It wasn't the first time or the last, but she liked it when the circumstances got out of hand—when wine helped them overcome their shyness. Then *Manolis*, alone or together with *Yusuf* and *Mehmet*, appeared out of nowhere to set the record straight. As had happened recently with that *French* agent, who, she was sure, was peeking on her as she prepared to go on stage. Only then the fight was not about her eyes but about the cunning twists of the dancers he brought to the nightclub. If it weren't for *Manolis*, the drunken sailors would have washed up the enraged agent in his attempt to save his girls. How elegantly, among so many wild people, he removed the

Frenchman, leaving him half-unconscious in a chair, as far away from the fray as possible. But what a pity that the commotion that night caused the stranger with the sweet accent to say goodbye to them so quickly. It was a pity because she had not had time, not to confirm that he was peeking while she was dressing, since she had no doubt about this, but to invite him to her dressing room next time his evil form would appear—she was more than certain of this too—again on the mysterious surface of the mirror. To show her his shirt and teach her some of the beautiful words he chewed so effortlessly as if they were spoon sweets.

Manolis took no more than a minute to bring her coat, perhaps delaying to turn off some forgotten light here or there in the great hall, but the way her thoughts chased each other's shadows that short interval seemed like eternity. She liked this young man and made no secret of it. In his black eyes, so clear, she had the impression that she could see the sea itself waving unhindered; that mighty companion which seemed to follow him everywhere, even to the bed to cover him when he slept. He spoke beautifully, as if the magic of the element found ways to whisper through his beautiful lips. He disarmed the other with his clear speech, and she, as a woman, found, in ninety-nine out of a hundred chances, her weapons powerless against him. Yes, and he might have keep turning his back on her at the first opportunity... but this small percentage, this one in a hundred, which for her was not a number but a window to the eternal gardens of spring, was enough to place him much higher on what her womanhood demanded than *Michael*. He said that hateful thing so beautifully: 'the boss asked you to get ready, *Leilah*!', his melodious voice pausing in her name as if he possessed the magic wand that she had failed to discern in the broomsticks of the people who filled their huge dustpans, crouching over them like the figures of a puppeteer.

He was perpetually turning his back on her yes, but not today! Today she felt it in his silence. Today was her day. And her fire, into which she would finally throw him again without any pity, lit as if it had never been extinguished! When *Michael* first introduced him to them, six or seven years ago, *Leilah* had looked meaningfully at *Mabruka*, unable to contain the spontaneous smile on her flushed cheeks—seeing in her fat friend's eyes reflected the same feeling mixed with awe. It was on one of his, literary nonexistent, visits to the kitchen of his property:

'*Manolis* will help you with whatever you need!' the dark man proudly declared, putting aside his favorite count for a while, letting the beads of his amber rosary fall silent tightly held in his fist. He had remained completely still, observing the two girls and the two henchmen, *Yusuf* and *Mehmet*, as if waiting to be congratulated on his find.

Leilah could not congratulate him then on his discovery, but she would gladly do so now, feeling the warmth of the coat slip into her numb body. He did not offer verbally to accompany her as he took the first steps, extending his arm around her waist to support her, as if to protect her from evil spirits or from the public servants with the wicker brooms and huge dustpans, the naïve wizard who would surely peek around hiding behind a barrel. A move that strongly reminded her of the tamers she had seen at the zoo feeding lions and other felines in iron cages.

She liked to compare the young henchman to the courageous tamers who were not afraid to enter the iron cages. Just as she would have liked to push the owner of the *Lido* nightclub there with her own hands, to finally bring him face to face with their sharp bloodthirsty teeth! To push him right there, while he was carelessly spinning his amber rosary! Oh, she was sure that she had seen him countless times watching them scared out there, entrenched in the safety that his position and big money gave him—just before the flames in the black holes of his eyes went out. 'The idiot!'

The flagstones went beneath her feet as she moved her weight from one to the other, carrying the same erotic swinging, the same sensuality that put on fire the elevated dance floor and took her revenge every night, captivating the patrons. Her husband abandoned her years ago invoking *Allah's* name three times, leaving her alone with two children, for the beautiful eyes of another woman. She had to survive. She remembered *Michael's* stepfather and his mother... She and her son had helped persuade the restaurant's then-owner to hire her.

'We need new people in the shop!' the old man had told her, waiting her to say yes, holding her hands tightly in his, looking appreciatively at her well-shaped body, leaving in the shadow the younger man who was also looking from a distance with his right hand resting on one of the tables.

The old man, *Leilah* recalled, did not want to turn the restaurant into a nightclub. But when he died, the very next day, the elevated dance floor suddenly sprang up in the middle of the hall, on the boards of which *Leilah* had shown from the beginning that she deserved her choice and the money they gave her. Yes, she had to make it, and the strangely beautiful woman with the red scarf opened up a completely different path for her with a simple wave of her hand.

'Look!' she said, pulling her away from the ghost of the old restaurateur, her son and the two waiters, *Yusuf* and *Mehmet*, so they wouldn't hear what he wanted to tell her.

'All those you see have come here for us, my dear!', her hand had remained suspended for a long time over the invisible heads of the men sitting at the tables.

'We shouldn't let them down, should we, *Leilah*?'

Her melodious voice flowed like gurgling water in the hot springs of the *Nile*, and just like her son's voice, her own voice clearly implied that there was no room for denial in what she was saying. No, they shouldn't have let them down, *Leilah* thought as her weight leaned vengefully on the arm of the young henchman, who could easily lift her into the air and carry her to the end of the destination and the few hundred meters remaining if asked.

The old *Egyptian* had died unannounced on a quiet summer night, while smoking his hookah calmly, withdrawn to his familiar place, on the edge of the table next to the entrance. The pipe between his frozen fingers was still smoking when he was discovered, pouring white fume out of its holes, encircling his expressionless face, moving upwards with small swirls before disappearing for good high, where the little bell cheerfully alerted him when someone pushed the front door.

The *Justice Department* official who arrived a few days after the burial had stood right there, holding a black briefcase in his hands, staring in disbelief at the people who had gathered around him to hear what he had to say. He had pulled out an incredible number of papers, putting them on the coffee table, before leaving the briefcase on one of the chairs.

'I request anyone who hears their name to declare it and sign on this paper,' he had pointed with the index finger of his free hand to the paper that stood out from the pile, pulling it lightly with the tip of his finger, lifting his gaze to see if he had been understood.

He had first of all mentioned the name of the woman with the red scarf, to continue with the rest, uttering clearly in *Arabic*: 'Michael... Leilah... Mabrouka... Yusuf... Mehmet...'

His world seemed to begin and end with these six people: his wife and the restaurant staff—the restaurant itself with its hundred tables and four hundred chairs. Even at that moment, when her husband's will was read, *Leilah* had not been able to discern anything false in this strange woman's behavior. Her grief, at the unexpected loss of the rich old *Egyptian*, seemed utterly real. In the depth of her eyes, since she happened to be next to her at that particular moment, *Leilah* would swear to see again the white swirls that the smoke of her master's hookah pour out when she first pulled his icy hands with hers! She shuddered at the power of the image that covered in a fraction of a second the gigantic distance of the past years.

The young henchman may not have had time to meet the woman who, like a spider, her web began to be woven around the old restaurateur's fortune from the first moment she set foot in the port of *Alexandria*, and *Leilah* believed that she owed more to her that she was among them today than to her son *Michael*. She was sure that she would have asked him long before he decided it on his own, perhaps foreseeing the quick end, leaving behind her the safe path that her son was happy to walk alone. Both *Mehmet* and *Yusuf* did not have time to satisfy the new modus operandi imposed by her plans, and episodes like this last one with the *French* agent were never absent, especially in the beginning, from drunk patrons looking for something more than the sensual spectacle. She remembered when she first took her up the elevated stage, there was still no electric light and she had hung from the ceiling as many lamps as she had found here and there, holding and shaking at an incredible pace a tambourine that had the *pyramids* and the sun painted on it.

'Well done *Leilah*!' she had shouted at her, tying her divine voice to the pauses of the blows. And when she came down, still dazed by the light scattered by the lit lamps that seemed to lower at the crazy pace of the rhythm to touch her bare belly:

'Well done dear, this is the way to keep men happy and I'm sure we won't disappoint them, will we?'

She would never forget the glow in the depth of her eyes, in which countless sparks swam as if fireworks had burst into the sky. Just as she would never forget the shivers that swept through her, seeing the white swirls of smoke in the same eyes, when the *Justice Department* official read the sections of the will. And her son had attended her first rehearsal, a few meters behind, without speaking or applauding. Just as he had watched his mother sign the covenant papers.

The old man had not forgotten anyone, and as much as *Leilah* had found it hard to believe what she was rushing to sign—the man with the briefcase had mentioned her own name, adding the word "apartment" in his crystal clear accent, then identifying with absolute precision the street and a host of other details she no longer remembered—the reality into which he had thrown everyone he wanted to remember him could not change. What had suddenly changed was her mood. Yes, men may not even be worthy to be spit on, but she was obliged to admit the fact that they did the most unlikely things just because they wanted to be remembered. And in this the old restaurateur seems to have done just fine, since whenever *Leilah* visited his grave, holding a bunch of flowers in her arms, she discovered, rather with pleasure, that someone else had managed to deposit his before her. But not all men are the same, she thought with a sigh, looking up at the profile of the young henchman who protected her from the rays of the rising sun. For example, who would like to remember or what did the owner of the *Lido* nightclub do to achieve this goal?

* * * * *

The young henchman, entering the dressing room, saw the long coat hanging forgotten in the open closet. The lights lit around the mirror, the scent of *Leilah's* sweaty body mixed with the scents of countless vials on the toilet, gave him the impression that the woman to whom they belonged had never left the small room. This light coat was always worn in the summers because, as she had explained: "I want to feel its warmth when I come home alone, it keeps me company and drives away evil spirits! You know, the world is full of these evil spirits! My husband..." She had started telling him a story in which her husband starred but had stopped almost immediately, incredibly annoyed with herself.

A sailor once told him a story about a mad emperor who set fire to an entire city just to dispel his boredom. With a sharp movement of his hand he turned off the electric light. Why shouldn't he possess similar power? He looked out of the corner of his eyes at his square shoulders, his strong arms. He was strong, yes very strong. Mr. *Michalis* had chosen him for this very reason among so many others. But his power could not be compared to the power of magic. Did his mother possess this strange power? He had not the slightest doubt about this, and as he carefully rested the coat on the wrist of his hand, he rushed to the exit. He walked like a blind man, without looking around as he would at other times to see if all things were in place. Through the fire, in the suffocating smoke of the burning city, *Leilah's* naked body had suddenly emerged on the elevated dance floor, mercilessly seeking his head on a platter.

Twelve

The sunlight came on this August morning as it did throughout the summer and winter when the clouds did not hide it with their shadow, from the large window of the bedroom. It was a relatively small room that communicated through a simple door with the rest of the apartment: the spacious living room, a second bedroom, the kitchenette and the simple bathroom. Located on the third floor of the low edifice, what made it stand out was precisely this window, the size of which was fully justified by the view of the endless blue of the sea.

When *Michael* first showed it to her, asking her in a hurry, well before they crossed the threshold of the entrance: 'What do you think? Well, what do you think?' She did not answer him right away. Yes, she did not answer him then, but much later, when the coolness of the northern sea breeze along with the colors of freedom that brought the island on which she was born so close to her that she could touch it if she stood for a while by the open window to rest her elbows on the windowsill—as she would later do sitting on the tall settee she had discovered among other furniture, assuming it was there for that very reason.

'It is amazing! It is great! Truly wonderful! I mean...' she had paused for a second or two, slowly directing her gaze back to where he was standing, perhaps wanting to temper her enthusiasm, to compensate for the disappointing account overall.

'The view is wonderful! Truly wonderful! I could have sat here for centuries!' and turning her head forward again she continued, as if inviting the reluctant owner of the *Lido* nightclub, who was standing a few meters behind, to come closer to her to see.

'Look, a huge liner and how many escorting little ones around it! One, two, three, four!', she had begun to measure emphatically the tugs around the large ship, perhaps guessing his weakness in counting.

But the trick had caught on and she had managed pulling him next to her. His huge back suddenly filled the scene, displacing her from the stage, and she heard him unsurprisingly confirm her arithmetic: 'One, two, three, four, indeed!'

Later, seeing the disappointment on her face, he had said to her:

'Don't worry *Maria*! This house is only temporary! Soon I will find the house you like, trust me!'

A whole year had passed, but they had not yet found that house. A fact that did not diminish her confidence in the least, since she understood that there were not many houses that were close to the *Lido* establishment and had the advantages of the small apartment, which had been given to them "for a low rent" by a "known friend". And for *Maria*, this reason mattered the most. Being at a distance of no more than a thousand steps—her husband had counted them accurately, and she had verified the fact, reasonably calculating that the forty or fifty extra steps were due to the difference in their pace. At the same time she found great satisfaction walking along the coastal promenade. Indeed, she found great satisfaction walking along the coastal promenade, chatting with the seagulls, not only from within but shouting and whistling as loud as she could, scaring the garbage collectors with the wooden brooms and the huge dustpans—as she used to do with the seabirds on the island when she went down with the other children to *Bouka* inlet.

One morning she had persuaded the owner of *Lido*, who had just returned from the nightclub, to walk there again.

'I want to see the sun at the edge of the sea!' she said, causing the flames grow in his fiery gaze.

As they approached, in the gray and colorless light of the night that was leaving, her gaze was drawn to the illuminated sign and, just below, in front of the front door, the figure of the young henchman with his arms crossed high on his chest seemed to support the whole edifice on the straight lines of his shoulders and back. Ready to repel pirates and smugglers who would dare to jump ashore, who would have the audacity to claim something from the gold that was definitely hidden somewhere.

She had advanced as if hypnotized for the last few meters, towards the light of the inscription where the insects of the night crowded around, falling on top of each other, abruptly ending their dark trajectories on the warm and hard surface of the lit lamps. The young henchman had remained in the same position, extinguishing a cigarette with a hasty movement of his foot—without covering with the singing colors of his deep voice the incessant, erratic and repulsive sound of the flying visitors.

Whenever she was near him, silence enveloped him like a mysterious cloud, and *Maria* would prefer him to talk to her openly—as he did with the girls in the kitchen, *Leilah* and *Mabruka*. To tell her the same stories, to make her laugh as they did, because she had secretly listened to him standing at the half-open door, restraining herself from breaking into the kitchen not because she did not think it was right but so as not to trap him in his silence again.

Silence frightened her. The prolonged silence brought with frightening clarity, with uncanny clarity, that night to the bedroom of the luxurious villa. But she would not let this nightmare bother her again, scare her now that the sunlight was coming in with the coolness of the sea through the open window. Her baby was sleeping in his cot and, resolutely pulling the double curtains against the window, she bent down and took him in her arms. But *Blacky* roamed freely in the garden at night, and that was certainly why the crickets stopped their hypnotic singing. She had pointed this out to the old coachman, telling him: '*Abdul*, if we tie up the dog, the crickets will keep us company at night...'

Poor *Abdul* listened to her and did her favors. Proof of this is that he went without asking for explanations to bring the key to the great gate. And when a little later he angrily banged his whiplash in the air, such was the clarity that things were happening around her, that she would swear that she had managed to discern the tip of the whip in the darkness flaring close, very close to the horse's muzzle. And his huge back, wrapped in the white *djellaba*, alleviated her wound as the carriage approached *Arais Street*, leaving behind, increasing with each rotation of the wooden wheels the distance separating them from the winemakers' villa.

His old wife had stood beside her in the small house at the edge of the garden, while *Abdul* was away to fetch the key. Frightened, she kept muttering some prayer to *Allah*, having understood exactly what had happened, studiously avoiding looking towards her. To get closer, to touch the torn nightgown, to throw at least some of her own garment to hide the invisible wounds on the naked limbs that still seemed to provoke, playing hide and seek with the trembling shadows. The rhythmic 'Klopp-kip-kip-Klopp' of the horse on the hard cobblestone seems to have frightened the crickets that night, because apart from this deafening sound *Maria* could not hear them singing the whole way. Just as she could not hear them singing for weeks afterwards on *Arais Street*, since every time they dared to start the horse's hooves with their repeated blows on the hard cobblestone, made sure to completely cover their lullaby.

She looked at herself in the large mirror she had brought along with other furniture when she moved from *Arais Street* to come to the third floor of the three-story edifice a few hundred meters from the *Lido* nightclub. Here the tragic cries of the white birds, with their calm and majestic flight during the day along with the night owls at night, had replaced the harsh sound of the horse petals. And although she still saw as clearly as she did that night, she could not put into words the tremendous change in her life in the months that followed. She had not heard the door open that night. The dark clouds lowering dangerously into the sky, the outbreak of the first lightning, the looming storm. She had not heard the footsteps of *Manolis Demestichas*, the wealthy heir to the winemakers' family, going up and down the villa's luxurious staircase. And when the dull sound of terrifying lightning reached her ears, lost among the pillows and covers, it was too late, too late to drive away the catastrophe.

From the very first days of her stay in the rich house of the heir of the winemaker family, she had understood the many problems in the relations of the husband and wife. And what she later learned from the mouth of aunt *Evangelia*, namely that as *Manolis Demestichas* himself claimed: "he opened the wrong door, thinking that he was opening the door of his own bedroom!" was... was... Her sharp thinking was momentarily disoriented despite the clarity, the terrifying clarity with which events approached her even now.

And if this postulate seemed close to the truth, for *Mary* it was nothing but a loathsome lie. In the darkness, before she lost consciousness, surrendering to the surprise and uncontrollable, almost fatal, clasp of his arms around her neck, she had managed to see in his eyes the torches of hell. And in the depth of his hellish soul, the figure burning in the fire that his favorite brandy *'Napoléon'* had helped to light was nothing like his wife's! When she descended the stairs of the luxurious staircase for the last time, holding with both hands the carved handrail so that she would not fall, full of strange disgust for her tattered nightgown, the light on the half-open door of his office clearly showed her that *Manolis Demestichas* was sitting there—as if nothing had happened. Sitting there in the leather armchair of his office with the crystal glass of his famous collection between his frozen fingers, opposite the bottle of his favorite brandy *'Napoléon'*. She had moved on quickly, constantly looking back, horrified by the clarity that hurt her as if she were staring straight into the sun, searching the ghost of *Abdul's* white *djellaba* that would lead her safely to her family home.

Aunt *Evangelia* had tried to justify him. She had never dared to speak to her directly, to touch the heart of the problem—something *Maria* would appreciate far more than any other approach. She told her about his weakness for drinking, about his troubled relations with his wife: 'I wanted to help him, just as I wanted to help you, my dear!' Abruptly releasing her hands and enumerating, using her fingers one by one for it, mentioning the surnames of her son's high and wealthy visitors and 'good friends'. Forgetting for a moment who she was talking to, forever shattering the last vestiges of goodwill she cherished of her father's venerable sister. And she would keep talking, putting aside the painful story: about the island, the house that needed repair, about the fact that they hadn't set foot there for years, and a bunch of disconnected chatter—without getting an answer from her niece who avoided even looking at her.

She had not seen her since that completely unknown doctor confirmed and verified scientifically what she sensed and which her father and aunt *Joanna* exorcised: 'The girl is expecting a child!' he had told them, bringing the agony back to their faces, postponing her frequent visits for the time being. She watched them and saw them accompany the doctor to the front door—the two women's light-colored dresses, on the side of her father's black costume, flourishing like joyful bells lowered from the church bell tower. The doctor bowing politely before the door closed in his face, waiting in vain for the traditional treat, the spoon sweet—sweet fig or sweet quince—that was common on such occasions.

And in the midst of this chaos, the truly terrifying clarity with which even the smallest details touched her, as if her own skin had suddenly been removed from the top of her head to her toes, a new, unprecedented, craven and guilt-filled feeling of triumph came to the surface! A strange feeling, perhaps similar to that of a castaway recovering in the sandy contact of the shore.

Her father approached her a few days after the visit of the *Egyptian* doctor and taking advantage of the truth that in a few months she would give birth to a child, he spoke vaguely to her about a man who was very interested not only in her own future but of the welfare of the whole family on *Arais Street*:

'You know, my dear... There is a very serious gentleman... I mean... You see, he talk to me about you when you were away from home, and I was waiting for you to come back to... In order to... But everything was lost from my mind after what...' He had stopped there, not daring to scrape the steaming blood on the open wound.

She had found funny the way her beloved father chose to bring her closer to the owner of the *Lido* establishment. His first words, which drew the red-painted velvet curtain and gently pushed her into the void. She had acknowledged the deepest pain in his expressive face, along with this huge moving mass behind the shadows in that totally unfamiliar mask. A mask that had managed to shake her even more than the red curtain, failing at that moment to capture the true dimensions, the obvious meaning. Indeed, this strange sensation dominated those moments, hiding or revealing—there was no real difference—the ways out.

But the solid ground was not at all able to stop her free fall into this mysterious void. And *Michael* was right there! The beads of his rosary fell silent as soon as her dress was seen in the small kitchen of their apartment, in the corridors or in the small office of the nightclub whose walls were covered from ceiling to floor with posters of 'artistic content'. The same was true when he smoked his cigarette, he extinguished it immediately by smearing the tablecloth with ashes, wobbling his hand on the ashtray with sharp movements up and down. She liked to hear him beat the amber beads, she easily deciphered their simplistic code, just as she deciphered his every move. There was a hidden force behind his unsmiling, always well-shaved face, behind his abrupt movements, in his long silences that were most often accompanied by the rattling of the beads of his amber rosary. A force upon which the control and polarization she felt she was exerting fascinated and flattered her immeasurably.

And yes, *Michalis* entered her life with the same momentum that *Manolis Demestichas* was crushed when he opened that 'wrong door' in his own house. At a time that really seemed to be far away, even though only twenty months had passed since they first met—lost in the labyrinthine corridors of everyday life, in the joys and expectations that the present and the future hide for each person individually. He entered her life resting on his square shoulders the four walls and the ceiling—holding for her sake the umbrella of heaven in its proper proportions.

This colossal force that seemed defenseless only when the swirling of her dress approached him; like a caress from a distance, forcing him into a movement reminiscent of the heads of parrots enclosed in cages. She was almost certain that he knew the child was not his. That he had discerned something at the bottom of the well had become obvious from the very first, indirect but with absolute sincerity, allusion to the possibility of becoming a father.

'How would you feel if we suddenly needed a baby cot?' she had asked him at an unsuspecting time, looking at him in eyes that had the strange characteristic: sometimes of shining like burning coals and sometimes of the sun disappearing at the edge of the horizon.

He had tried to tell her something, but she had not been able to contain his words. Yet the edge of the horizon was there. In the round pupils of his eyes the light was extinguished like the flame of candles in the candelabra in the strong wind that enters unannounced from the door of a church. Could he have learned the truth through his contacts, from his numerous 'friends' or from a stranger who by chance, in *Demestichas'* circle, had information? She could not guess. How could she know if he did not make a start, if he did not take the lead and clear up her secret?

But *Michael* had made sure to allow room for her, in that strange way of men who, even when next to and behind each other, know how to retreat to win, if not the war, at least a battle. Taking care sometimes more successfully and sometimes less, not to disturb her, though unable to hide the flickering of his eyelids, the extinguishing of the warmth he generally radiated and its replacement with that of frozen pretense, of artfully guided indifference every time he came close to the newborn creature.

She was silently grateful to him for this precious space. His given submissiveness had helped heal faster from her fall into that mystical void. A won battle, yes, for the owner of the *Lido* nightclub. She could acknowledge this, just as she had acknowledged the hidden graces of the silent man, which made even the possibility of a happy life not far from reality, if his weaknesses did not cast a threatening shadow, putting a brake on any expectations, fueling a constant anxiety. For she had seen him many times in the small office of the nightclub counting the paper pounds, over and over again, rubbing adoringly between his fingers the printed surface of each note separately, before binding them in bunches and locking them in the safety of the small safe, on the wall behind his back. In those moments she had failed to get his attention, and as his lips formed the numbers, one behind the other: 'one, two, three... one, two, three!' the shadows of anxiety gathered like black clouds on the ridges of the mountains of *Kasos*. Her father had borrowed money from the owner of the *Lido*! She did not know the exact amount, but that did not matter much. What bothered her were the well-founded suspicions that money and the lifeless numbers formed on *Michael's* lips were behind the approach.

But these weaknesses were not capable, at least for the time being, of hurting her, and his behavior had finally succeeded in relaxing her suspicious mind. And *Leilah*, the nightclub dancer, more than once in their conversations in the kitchen had directly referred to her boss.

'Well, my dear, tell us now about the exploits of our beloved bull!' she had asked—surprising *Mary* that was not prepared for such games with the staff, and had hurried to finish:

'Don't be afraid, my dear! This man has never had and will never have eyes for another woman...' She then recounted as many details as she remembered about the various bands that passed by and "about which the posters of women on the walls of his office speak for themselves"—repeating twice, with the same emphasis, her concluding phrase:

'Well, believe me or not, he never reached out to touch one of the lassies who paraded in here!'

Leilah's manner was not utterly outrageous, and *Maria* had remained seated opposite her on one of the wooden stools, next to the bottle and ready food counters, smiling awkwardly, grasping with both hands her bloated belly that could be seen despite the extra width of the well-trimmed dress.

On their walks along the promenade, walking beside her without holding her hand, squeezing the amber rosary instead in his fists of muteness, he had told her about his stepfather. The old *Egyptian* restaurateur resembled in his narratives the brush and canvas for his mother's portrait. But the painting remained unfinished all these months. He had never told her about his real father, nor had he given details of his life before *Alexandria*, except for a brief description of embarking "on the big ship in the port of *Piraeus*" bound for the vast country of the *Nile* "where giant palm trees could be seen many miles before the ship turned into the breakwater..."

Maria knew very little about *Piraeus*. She knew the harbor more from her father's descriptions than from the pictures that stayed with her the only time she set foot there. She had dared to ask *Michael* about this other port, but he had looked at her half-closing his eyes, his hermetically closed mouth unsmiling—preferring, instead of an answer, lowering his head and gaze, to enigmatically twist his amber rosary before turning his back on her and walking away, shifting his feet on the wooden planks of the small apartment, a prelude to his lonely exit to the coastal promenade.

But the clarity with which things were coming at her allowed her to see every detail painfully, the fine grains of dust settling everywhere—in the alleys and stairs that led to the charmingly lit windows of small, detached houses. There she could see, behind *Michael's* mother's dress and in the mighty swirling wind behind her, other men crowding like bees around the queen, each claiming questionable paternity on his behalf. Yes, it was very easy to complement with the missing colors the unfinished painting and the rattling at the beating of the beads on the sharp rotations of his rosary, his hermetically closed lips on the seemingly indifferent face, the lowering of his head, his square back silently moving away, the shaking of his feet on the wooden boards of the small apartment, offered her the best brushes to apply them.

Thirteen

In June, when the seagulls left the sea to fly low, over the rooftops of the first houses, looking for a safe place to lay their eggs, the young henchman of the *Lido* establishment was ordered to look for a dance troupe—one of the dozens that constantly changed hangouts in the world of the night. It was a hot morning like now, the second time the dark man approached him with the same purpose, three months later. The beautiful wife of the owner of *Lido* was enjoying the shade of a crude awning, which he had set up with the help of the other two henchmen.

The crude awning was about twenty steps away from the main entrance of the nightclub and so many more from the stone wall with the openings, the stone steps and the first marble stalls. Next to her stood the boss, in a picture so familiar over the past few months that it no longer surprised anyone, before deciding to perform the equally familiar movement of spinning around his heels, to head towards him with the momentum of the freed bull in the dusty arena. He had stopped abruptly in front of him, creating the impression to those who did not know his intentions that the coming collision would flatten the man who remained unperturbed in his position.

'Listen, *Manolis*, it is time to do something! We cannot allow this to continue, do you hear? We have left things to chance all these months, and this must end. *Leilah* is very tired...' he had begun to tell him, keeping his head slightly bowed, parallel to the rest of his body, arms hanging freely downward, the pupils of his eyes facing upwards.

'*Leilah* said she is very tired of this situation, as are we, and the people who do us the honor of sitting at the tables every night!'

'Do you hear me *Manolis*? People who come every night are tired of seeing the same things and *Leilah* told *Maria* that she feels very tired! I can't understand why she didn't tell me directly, but she preferred to tell my wife! Perhaps because a woman communicates better with another woman than with a man!'

A pair of tiny flashes had furrowed the deep and inscrutable bottoms of his eyes, sounding like a bright echo every time the word woman formed on his tight lips.

'I decided to give you the opportunity to search... to find...'

The long pauses between words, his direct reference to inactivity along with the attitude of the charging bull in front a red cloth, had made him feel extremely uncomfortable, despite the feeling that what he had been waiting for years would finally come true.

'Yes, that is my decision *Manolis*. But it is more than that... It is my confidence that you will make it, that you will succeed!'

The same pair of small flashes had again lined the inscrutable depth in the pitch-black pupils, under the broad and unfurrow forehead—this time accompanying his last word, having thus taken care to imply that he left no room for failure.

'I will do what I can, Mr. *Michael*! I want you to trust me! I will do everything in my power!'

The owner of *Lido* had not sat down to listen to more and performing the same comic pirouette he had walked away with the same determination with which he had approached him.

And for *Manolis* it was not at all difficult to carry out his mission. In the almost camouflaged and otherwise faceless entrance leading to *Giorgio's* dark office, the inscription with his name carved on an oval bronze blade, bent in a press so that it protruded from the wood of the door like a large shell, described just this: *'Giorgio Armadino'*. Leaving out everything else that would be discovered by those who would ring the little bell on the side of the door, or knock directly on the wood, if they happened to prefer this way than to pull the short cord on the right side of the freshly painted wall. And this bell was rung only by individuals of prestige and a lot of money.

'Manolis! Ha, ha, ha! How long have it been since I last meet you?'

The *Italian impresario* had his feet resting on the edge of his desk, lost in the back of his sophisticated armchair, holding a glass in his left hand and a cigarette in his right. A cigarette seemingly forgotten, judging by the size of the ash at its end, which far exceeded the length of the remaining paper wrapper, and which had managed to fall before he pulled his legs to stand up.

Manolis had crossed the threshold of this place several times in the near past, either carrying a message 'on behalf of Mr. *Michalis*', or as a visitor, without any professional reason—just to enjoy the frozen *'martini'* and the *'European sigaretta'* along with the pleasant, 'really enjoyable' company of the *Italian impresario.*

Giorgio Armadino had stood up unceremoniously, trying to command his uneconomical height—well exceeding six feet if his thin skeleton was not hunched over slightly, recalling the curled inscription on the front door. Wrapped in his elegant dark suit, his jacket with the double rows of buttons right and left, always buttoned to perfection, accentuated his waist as if he had been cut in two by a rusty imitation of *Excalibur.* The black bow tie, high on his neck, gave him a comical note as it was tightly pulled on the collar of his immaculate white shirt, where the same weapon seemed to have touched him, giving the impression that his head remained in place by some miracle.

Manolis had in mind at least ten or twelve other people who did the same job as *Giorgio* and who, depending on how much each nightclub owner was willing to entrust to them, promised to compensate them with something new. It was obvious that the last thing a good *impresario* wanted was to fool these people. But *Giorgio* was his man. 'The prettiest women love *Giorgio*, they trust him,' he would tell him at the first opportunity—changing his seating position perpetually, alternating up and down his legs, bending forward, or lifting himself up as he straightened his body backwards. But his success lay not so much in the fact that he was loved and trusted by the most beautiful women, as in the fact that he had managed to be trusted by their agents and consequently by the directly unsatisfied, utterly greedy, shop owners.

The last job *Giorgio* booked with the owner of *Lido* was none other than that unfortunate deal, where the protagonist was the *Frenchman* in the plush shirt. *Manolis* had tried to explain to him that *Michael* did not blame him for the unexpected departure of the irritable *Gaul*.

'It is not your fault that this rocking *lulu* couldn't control his nerves at the teasing of those drunken *Englishmen*. You should have been there to see him...'

'Yes, you should have seen him fighting alone, yelling at them while everyone waited their turn to push him into the circle they had formed! Always polite these *Englishmen*, believe me, never touched him two at the same time and the *Frenchman* seemed capable of anything! If it was up to me I would let the fight continue until the end, but in such cases my position is really very difficult, you know...'

But his honest performance, such selfless support, had not been enough to remove his friend's melancholy.

'Whatever you say to me, I understand that *Michalis* is very sad with me! Very sad! Months go by, huh, and he doesn't ask for my help, huh? How do you explain that, *Manolis*, huh?'

And *Manolis* understood that the only solution that would finally put things in their place was the one that the inamorato owner of the nightclub had let drift without doing anything, completely outside of what he was used to doing, and which alienated more than anyone else the people who worked near him. The temptation was great in the moments when the good *impresario* leaned over his ringed waist to offer one of the fragrant *sigaretta*, pushing his sophisticated arm-chair backwards, putting forward the subtle bond of their friendship, the open snuff box between his long fingers, to speak openly about what he believed was behind *Michael's* annoying inaction.

But he had not dared to do so, not because he was afraid, but because he respected the change in his behavior more than anyone else. *Giorgio*, who had attended his wedding sur-rounded by five or six "beautiful *ragazze*," could not have as-sumed that the focus of inaction lay in this very event. For the gentle *impresario* the opposite sex was something like salt and pepper in his food, something like the soil under his shoes and the clear or cloudy sky above his head.

Manolis had seen these women for the first time the mo-ment the *Italian* introduced them to him on the huge plat-form, the last step of the other thirty-two, where the groom waited for the bride before they disappeared into the dark in-terior of the church. Apart from his parents, he had two boys and his wife who waited patiently for him on the other side of the *Mediterranean*. He had shown him family photographs, which he carefully locked together with other personal doc-uments in his drawers, but for him the beautiful sex was like the flowers that adorned the edge of his desk, making sure to change them as often as he changed the last along with the wa-ter in the crystal vase.

'Take a look, *Manolis*! This is *Gregorio*, my big guy! And that's *Giorgino*, the little one, uh, and my wife among them, huh!' He had shown them to him when in his dark office three female figures could be seen half-naked from the half-open door leading to the small bedroom.

He had not managed to surprise the *Italian impresario* at all, when he announced that this time he was not conveying a message "on behalf of Mr. *Michalis*"—that he had not come to pass the time pleasantly, but that he was coming to put an end to the long inactivity that "has so tired us all in *Lido*..."

'That's good, very good *Manolis*!' he responded him with due seriousness to form and support the vowels at the tip of his tongue, managing at the last minute to throw the ashes of his cigarette into one of the two, full to the round rim, luxurious ashtrays.

'One has to trust the people he works with, huh? And you're doing it there... How many years, huh?' He had hung his head back, trying to remember how many years he had known the young henchman of the *Lido* nightclub, changing the subject as soon as he returned to his usual position, sucking and hurriedly blowing the smoke between his teeth.

'These days there are many opportunities, eh, *Manolis*... Many opportunities!' he said, leaving his cigarette in the safety of the semi-round recess, having again lowered his feet to the floor, before pulling from the central drawer some pictures caught with an iron paper clip on the cover of a notebook.

'Here, check these...' he showed him a couple of pictures, drawing his fingers on the sheets of the open notebook.

'I suggest these dancers to be fixed. They are from *Syria* and have not been in *Alexandria* for over a month. The first, and until now last shopkeeper, was so pleased that he invited me to watch the show! Let *Michael* say yes and arrange an artistic mantra for you. They are very good *Manolis*, huh! Very good, huh!'

Manolis had remained hesitant, confused not only about what he would choose, but about whether he would delay, whether he should consult the owner of the *Lido* establishment, carried away by that 'let *Michael* say yes...' But there was absolutely no room for booboo. It was obvious that there was no room for delay, no back and forth, no advice in this direct award, which left open the possibility of failure. And *Manolis*, showing his confidence in the *Italian impresario*, had finally agreed with him that "the *Syrian* girls" would take it upon themselves to revive the withered *Lido*.

'Oh, don't be afraid, *Manolis*, eh! *Giorgio* rarely makes mistakes, eh! Don't be afraid! And don't forget, huh! *Giorgio* watched show and was satisfied, huh! The shop will be full of people and the only thing I'm curious about is how long they stay in *Lido*, uh, ha, ha, ha!'

Giorgio's proposal to close the deal with the *Syrian* girls proved successful. The five girls, with their white skin and black hair, had managed to impress everyone, but most of all the demanding owner of the nightclub. On stage they alternated one after the other, to continue their dance, constantly increasing their number on the elevated dance floor, until all five appeared together at the end. A performance that was very cleverly staged, acted in a kind of beauty contest and in which the audience was invited at the end to nominate the queen of the evening. *Michael* kept the numbers in his mind:

'one, two, three, four, five'! It was easier for him than remembering their names.

'I don't know which one is the prettiest, but what I can say is that the tables are so divided that I would vow, if they didn't go out on the dance floor together, that the five girls are but one!' he said suddenly, without waiting for an answer from the lips of *Manolis* who had rushed to his urgent nod.

Ahmed had printed under his own instructions the slips of paper, which for almost ten weeks had advertised the performance, and which had become the occasion for *Leilah* to express her opinion:

'You are a fool *Manolis*! So what do you think people will come to see the spectacle or vote for the most beautiful girl?' The two of them stood under the protection of the crude awning, he hunched over, since his height did not allow him otherwise, in the shade of a scorching sun—an awning made of thick canvas, similar to the one covered in the holds to keep away the rain from the precious cargo, tied with strong string to four wooden stakes tucked into four permanent openings in the ground. *Leilah* had returned the printed paper to him by shaking her head, resting both hands on her thin waist. A move not so ostentatiously negative in itself if it were not accompanied by the unflattering comment and the voice full of poison:

'You must be very stupid if you really believe that people, instead of seeing what is happening around them, will sit and fill in crosses next to names! Very stupid!'

Later, when during breaks the patrons happily devoted their time playing with the little pencils, he could see the frustration growing in *Leilah's* ill-conceived face. And he felt sorry for her when he saw her watching from the half-open kitchen door—she held one of the two sheets slightly open with her hand so that she could see without being seen—the progress of the performance. The musicians playing not for her, not for her dance, but for other women—*Allah* only knew how much longer! And *Tarek*, the "great *Tarek*" as the *Syrian* agent introduced himself, camouflaged like a huge *chameleon* in his baggy clothes so that no one would recognize his *Jewish* origins, sat at the secluded table next to the owner of the *Lido*, listening to every movement around him, watching the show seemingly unperturbed.

'This... the... This... *Tarek*, didn't he tell us what his name is? Well, he reminds me of a snake lurking in the grass for its victims!' *Leilah* told him more than once.

'He must be much worse than *Michael*! I think he must hate women! He never walked out of my dressing room, never deigned, except on the first day when he bowed like a theater-goer in front of me, to look at me again!

Perhaps *Leilah* was right in what she said, but *Manolis* had not—until that moment—collaborated with a dance group which, apart from the unusually good discipline for the standards of the *East*, managed to surprise in a different way each night. And if *Michalis* had known in advance how things would turn out, he would have asked for a much longer duration in the contract he signed with *Tarek*. In addition, the price *Tarek* had agreed with the young henchman had come as a big surprise to the owner of the nightclub.

Manolis did not know, and probably would never know, whether the strictness of the *Egyptian* port authorities was what led the 'great *Tarek*' to bend over the seal and rest the index finger of his right hand on the still fresh ink at the bottom of the paper, or whether his devotion to extinct practices was responsible for this.

'Dear sir,' he had begun to say to him, as the index finger of his right hand had not yet had time to pull, seeming to enjoy not only the touch of the imprinted eagle facing west but also the smell of ink, moving his gaze slowly upwards and fixing it high in *Manolis* gaze.

'We may never have met before, but this is not the first time I have come to *Egypt*. I must tell you that the authorities here are doing a very good job, a very good job. No matter how you look at it! Either on your side or on ours!'

He had a tendency, in his stunningly beautiful *Arabic* accent, to double down a portion of the words within his sentence—as if he found in it something of the pleasure of someone petting an animal, mimicking the movement of his hand to the words swirling on his palate and, accordingly, the ears of the man with whom he had the honor of conversing.

The *Syrian* agent, camouflaged in his loose clothes like a huge *chameleon* coming down from tree branches to walk the streets, had managed to fool *Manolis* on at least one occasion. When *Giorgio* first showed him his papers, he noticed in the brackets the number '71', which was confirmed in full by the words 'seventy-one years old', automatically diminishing the meaning of the other elements of his description. This figure had made it difficult for him to believe that the man opposite him was the same man who appeared in the descriptions and official papers of the *Italian impresario*—because he actually looked, if not thirty, at least twenty years younger—and leaving aside his remark about the *Egyptian* authorities he was tempted to ask:

'Forgive me the rudeness, but it's real, I mean is the age I read in the reports correct? Are you really seventy-one years old?'

A subtle smile had blossomed on the *Syrian* agent's lips, a faint smile of satisfaction, perhaps betraying that this same question he must have been asked to answer on other occasions before. Slightly taller than average, with proportions that would be envied by much younger men than him, his baggy clothes could not hide his athletic body. The pure white hair, along with the white mustache, would keep pace with his age if it were not so thick and well-groomed, as happens even in young people who turn white for some reason prematurely.

'Every woman feels happy before such a compliment, but the same is true, my dear, of every man!' he had replied, the glow of his astonishingly white teeth mocking not the number of seventy-one years but the very nature of things and the decay that wants to inexorably turn iron into rust, leading to resignation, apathy and death.

'What you read is absolutely right, my dear friend, why would I want to hide my age? There is no reason, there is no reason. Believe me, no, no reason at all!'

Yes, this *chameleon* had come after almost two years of inactive monotony to the *Lido* nightclub and had left after sixty days. Indeed, he had finally left, leaving behind the stamp of a successful collaboration, which of course was credited to the young henchman. His five 'girls' may not have had the freedoms that the *French* dancers had—nor was their escort as liberal as his *French* colleague—but they had managed to confuse even the terrible count of the demanding nightclub owner, where the sums were completely satisfactory.

'Listen to me *Manolis*!', the owner of *Lido* was again next to his young henchman.

'The result was very good. It's a shame you didn't get a longer term, but that's okay. Listen to me *Manolis*, you know me better than anyone! You know I don't like too much talk. Well, we must be careful not to stand idly by again. All right? *Giorgio's* office is waiting for work, and so are the other offices. I want you to look for *Tarek's* replacements as quickly as possible! If possible as early as tomorrow!' He left him again, without waiting for an answer, executing the familiar spin, briefly hiding the perspective towards the crude awning and the girl with the long black hair, where the jerks of his legs carried him swiftly reminiscent of the movement of the compass in the abrupt change of course of a ship.

Manolis was sure that the girl with the long black hair had seen him hurriedly throw away the cigarette and extinguish it with his shoe, while *Michalis'* back was oriented towards the opposite route and he would have liked, now that he was alone again, to light a second cigarette, sensing that this move would not go unnoticed. He could have done it because, as in other times, the boss had his attention turned away from the nightclub, facing now his wife and the great expanse of the sea—but he was content to cross his arms high on his chest again.

The excruciatingly blinding light of the sun that rose to its zenith this August morning, the heat from the reflection on the concrete ground, was made bearable by the light north wind that carried with it the freshness of the open sea, diffusing it everywhere in the splendor of the day. Under this light, *Manolis* could see the air on the thick canvas and, beneath it, on *Maria's* dress—the same air he breathed and which he found particularly pleasant. In the afternoon, or at the latest by the next morning, he would try to make contact with the *Italian impresario* again. The female figures, in *Giorgio's* half-dark bedroom, were mingled with the alarming cries of two huge seagulls, who decided to suddenly give up their rest on the steps, in the stone openings, and entrust the opening of their amazing wings to the freedom of the big sky. And if he was absent, then he would be looking for someone from the rest. Yes, he was happy that his boss had entrusted him with the management of the nightclub for the second time, and as his mind seemed to clear with this thought, with confident movements, he placed a new cigarette on the edges of his lips. He lit it and let the smoke mingle with the slight north wind, the tragic cries of seagulls, who were still hovering a few dozen feet above his head.

Fourteen

The owner of the *Lido* nightclub had never felt the ground more solid, the air so clear, the sounds so vivid and meaningful around him. Like, for example, the cries of two seagulls who, for some unknown reason, insisted for a while on making the same circle, again and again, climbing a few meters high, before descending lower again with their wings spread out—as if they were testing their strength against the blinding light of the bright day, constantly moving their heads in a way that would be more suited to lords or kings, in their effort not to greet the crowd below, but to let nothing escape them in the ever-changing perspective on this reconnaissance flight.

Yes, there were times when, surprising even himself, he could discern some odd details that had never before troubled his thinking. These moments, it is true, did not last long. For how could they hold more than a blink of an eye when all things around him had this solid form? Firmly and unwaveringly appearing in their place, a condition that by its very nature urged anyone who felt them to put one number next to another. Anyone could count them, thus mathematically proving their indisputable existence. And that was a real relief, every time he landed to shake his legs in a perfectly specific direction, where everything was ready to welcome him without any intention of surprise.

He was very pleased with his young henchman, *Manolis*, though he had left him at the entrance of his property, without patting him on the shoulder, without saying anything nice, hurrying to suppress any positive feeling. He was, however, more pleased with himself than with his henchman. For he felt, as he whirled his own words over and over again, that the way he had chosen was the right way, the way that would ensure his respect first of all. As simple as, say, the number four, as many as the stakes that held the crude awning, the canvas tied with thick string at their ends. But there he could go no further, for under the protection of the cool shade, which stretched like the hand of God on the hard ground, the figure of his wife could not fit or, worse, be described even if he had all the books of arithmetic at his disposal.

There, in the warmth of the summer morning that was moving relentlessly forward, under the gray fabric of the crude awning, her sideways gaze met his. Like the swords of two gladiators and it seemed to him that, as happens in a real confrontation where one of the gladiators attacks and the other defends, it was she who defended, although the sword—he could already feel it slipping unchecked away from him—that had the best chance of falling was his rather than hers!

It was a strange feeling. Strange, yes, but at the same time so pleasantly real! A feeling that seemed to have the power to put aside, to absorb with incredible ease the annoying tremors of a possible defeat. Yes, there she stood next to him, in the handful of protective shade, without her appearance having changed at all in the last twelve months—giving him, however, the impression of a completely different creature from the one he had first met on the same coastal promenade, recognizing at her side *Nikolas*, the *Greek* tailor who occasionally repaired his suits. But even under this bright light of early maturity in their relationship, he could not capture and put his emotions in order—accurately count his steps in the green, yet filled with all the other colors, landscape of spring in his life.

Until now he had not been able to explain, and seriously doubted if he would ever explain, what it was that pushed him to follow this path. He was not a man who would unnecessarily show much interest in learning details about others. No, he was not a gossipmonger at all, and those who knew him well could attest to that. His favorite henchman *Manolis* for example, *Yusuf* and *Mehmet* as well. Everyone who knew him well. His only weakness—he would never admit to being a defect—was, of course, his numbers, his counting.

He could count and recount the banknotes, take them together in bundles, count the bundles, put them on top of each other forming small towers, finally place them in the same formations in the safe, in his small office, without getting tired in the least. Indeed, his weakness in counting, and his lustful recognition of the power of money, was more than a given. He had lists, he admitted it. Lists of 'customers' where, next to the names, date and amount borrowed by each of them, there was the necessary signature—irrefutable proof of its validity. On one of these lists was *Nikolas'* name. But the owner of the

Lido establishment could have sworn that he knew nothing more about his family, except for the little information necessary to secure the payment of the loan. Like, for example, that *Nikolas* was a tailor and came from *Kasos* island. That his father, before he died, excelled from a managerial position in some important post in the construction of the *Suez Canal*. That he had left him a three-story house on *Arais Street* and that the tailor's shop was on the ground floor, a few meters away from the *café* with the 'number seven'. That *Nikolas* had a sister, a sister much older than him, married to a very rich merchant and winemaker whose name escaped him...

'Wasn't my idea for the awning good? Look *Michael*! Everyone can sit here as long as they want without the risk of being sunburned!' *Maria* told him as she allowed herself to lie on the striped cloth of a *chaise longue*. And she was right, since the entertainment club—built to operate at night—did not have such commodities, if one excluded the stone wall, the steps and the marble stalls along the brow of the shore, whose protection against the attacks of blinding light was limited and offered only to dogs and cats who fit comfortably in the small corners, in the cool recesses, adjacent to the embrace of the sea.

His wife was still staring at him from the comfortable *chaise longue*, no longer sideways or as defensive as it seemed at first, as if seeking his own consent to the ridiculous awning affair. A case that under other circumstances he would have passed by without even answering if he had been asked what he thought of it by other people—*Leilah*, say, or *Tasia*, the *Muslim* cleaner who swept the shop in the mornings. This was another strange surprise—the little lies he was forced to tell in response to such trivial matters, as if he were taking the side of a dangerous spirit so as not to displease it.

'And, look *Michael, Manolis'* thought of digging permanent openings so that the stakes can come out and come in whenever we want was very clever, what do you think?'

Michael remained silent against *Maria's* lowered shields, letting the beads of his rosary answer—as if to exorcise the evil spirits, the almost human cries of the two seagulls, their insistence on constantly hovering over the makeshift awning. This woman had a son! *Evangelia* was her name, and he remembered it precisely because the meaning of the words that made it up amounted to 'good news'. As she herself pointed out to him on the steps of the church, looking at him from the height of five feet eleven of her excessively obese body, making him wonder how the thin spear-like heels on her black shoes could withstand such weight.

Yes, this imposing woman had an only son. *Nikolas* had introduced him to him one day at the entrance of the port authority, when the three of them were there for different reasons. In one of these coincidences, which make the whole world seem so small that could fit into the few square meters of the customs building that took care of the safety and proper operation of the port. 'This is my nephew...' He had conveyed without much arrogance, seeming to want to avoid introductions. *Manolis Demestichas*—his name had remained in his memory because they had worked together in the past, before learning in their joint meeting in the lobby of the port authority that he was *Nikolas'* nephew—had looked at him behind the permanent fog that moistened the eyeballs of his colorless eyes as if he was seeing him for the first time in his life. Their cooperation had been abruptly interrupted due to a trivial, literally silly misunderstanding, for which: "Mr. *Demestichas* bore no responsibility whatsoever". As *Michalis* himself had admitted in front of the winemakers' successor and the repetition of the phrase in their last meeting, having solemnly failed to bring to mind the scene of the termination of their cooperation, had surprised the owner of *Lido* who never forgot things related to professional teamwork. And now, as then, in front of the puzzled figure of *Nikolas'* nephew, the sound of the beads of the amber rosary had helped him overcome the difficulties that seemed to be outside the limits of his simplistic arithmetic.

But then this girl had played a game against him or, more correctly, she was the protagonist in the game that was set up against him. Yes, yes, the protagonist in a dirty game! A dirty game in the throes of which he found himself, strangely of his own volition. A dirty game at his expense! A matter of fact that is absolutely incredible! Yes, a dirty game against him, and in truth the persistent sound of the repeated spins of the rosary, between the thick fingers of his right hand, meant nothing more than that he was ready to ask her *carte blanche* the question that had risen to tyrannize him. Instead, perhaps because he did not wish to debunk the various scenarios he had worked out in his mind, he said, leaning even further over the young woman's lying body:

'Manolis...' He pointed with a sharp movement of his head at the young henchman, who had just lit a new cigarette and was crossing his arms high on his chest.

'Manolis is doing fine with the management of the night-club. I am very pleased with him... The last job he booked with that *Syrian* agent brought people back to the tables. I should had taken you with me one night to watch one of the shows. We haven't had such success for years! Too bad they didn't sit with us longer, too bad!'

Her answer was lost in the almost human cries of the two seagulls, who apparently had not yet decided to move away from the point where the makeshift awning seemed to be the most important target closest to the coastal promenade and the sea. An answer that he would not have heard anyway since he had spoken only to break his own silence, to ease the weight of his miserable uncertainty.

But, no, he would not try to learn the truth now from this creature who looked so fragile, so defenseless, and who had been tied to the chariot pulled by his own horses in a way that had truly impressed him. If what he vaguely assumed could have happened was indeed happening, then there were other ways to find out the truth. His young henchman, for example, who did so well with the management of the nightclub, why wouldn't he do just as well if he was tasked with looking for the end of the tangled knot? The idea was pushed away, extinguished like the flames of the candles in the candelabra of the church in the abrupt puffing of the lamplighter. How was it possible to involve *Manolis* in this... in this highly personal affair?

No, there was absolutely no way he would ask anyone for help in this matter! He moved back a whole step, as if he wanted to cancel his thoughts, to exorcise the evil spirits who were pushing him to make mistakes, pushing him to fall to the nearest precipice. *Nikolas'* words may have hidden the heavy secret. In the common denominator of his father-in-law's general attitude, from beginning to end, towards his proposal, there was a change, a change that resulted in the ease with which things went their way from one point onwards.

And on this path, which changed his life the way it changed it and gave birth to a child who was not his own, the common denominator was there—being a number below the numbers he valued so much, and which division made seem unrecognizable, almost repulsively frightening. He felt it, he could feel it even now, let's say in the end, that he was still unwanted in the family of the tailor from *Kasos* island. *Nikolas'* nephew, the wealthy heir to winemakers, had not deigned to come to his wedding!

For some inexplicable reason the figure of this colorless man persisted in becoming entangled in the realm of his imagination, playing with the reality of the blinding morning light, the shadows on the lying figure on the *chaise longue*, and the creepy screams of the two seagulls over the gray canvas of the makeshift awning. And it may have been true that once, in the relatively near past, due to a trivial, literally foolish misunderstanding, the cooperation between them broke down—just as it was true that since then they have never had any other professional approach or contact—but this was not such a serious reason as to justify the distances that the honorable successor had kept then and still did to this day. And then his wife was in his own house when *Nikolas* tried to reassure him. And the *Greek* tailor had kept his word, since he did come, even though it took three whole months for it.

But the man who sat across from him that night in the nightclub seemed to have come straight from hell rather than any other place, only to let him know the pleasant fact that his beloved daughter was agreeing to marry him! Yes, yes, *Nikolas'* movements were now easy to palpate, to line up, to line up like soldiers in line, prey to the rigid captain's strict inspection.

That night had gone by quietly. *Leilah* had danced three times in front of a demanding audience of *Jewish* sailors. He found him sitting at his usual table, facing the entrance of the nightclub so that when the bell rang he would not even have to turn his head. The time that has elapsed since their last meeting was so long and his uncertainty so inflated that he fully justified the fleeting upset of the person to whom he had confided, he considered it more a confession than anything else, his proposal.

It was a momentary and unpleasant feeling, yes, but not at all unprecedented, since his profession by nature constantly imposed such emotions and surprises. But the look of the tailor from *Kasos* island said it all! He had been so horrified by the sight of *Nikolas* at the other end of the table that he had spontaneously drawn his gaze away, sweeping the clientele for the first time since entering the large hall of the establishment. The outcome was, nevertheless, positive! But what lurked at the bottom of the dark well of which he had lifted the lid, and which was in danger of proving heavier than his strong hands could hold? He had to find out, he had to clear up the case, and there was no power in the world capable of preventing him from doing so.

In the perspective, a large ship was approaching the break-water. On her deck he could easily discern even from this distance, using the binoculars he had bought at a very good price from some *American* sailors, a part of the crew on alert. Four people on the wings of the bridge. Two in front of the bow, one on the right side and the other on the left, approximately in place of the large openings from where the half-lowered chains with anchors would be released at the temporary anchorage, until an empty pier was found in the harbor. Four or five more at the stern, with their elbows resting on the salty rails. Behind the square windows of the bridge the captain would let the *Egyptian* pilot direct the helmsman in his broken *English* as soon as the ship turned at breakwater: 'Keep it straight now! *Starboard* ten! Dead slow! Dads it, dads it... Alright, good job, good job!' And down in the engine room and the other compartments the rest of the crew, who would bring the total number to twenty, perhaps twenty-five people, enough to fill the chairs and tables of the nightclub.

Hiding behind the powerful lenses of his binoculars, he momentarily came to say to his wife: '*Maria*, look, a ship is entering the port! See! We need to find *Tarek's* replacement soon, because otherwise I'm afraid we'll lose customers!' Mostly to distract her from the poles and the makeshift awning, his henchman's clever idea of digging permanent openings so they could get out and in with ease, but he restrained himself from doing it firstly because he thought it was not something that would catch her interest and secondly because he did not want to annoy her, since he realized that in the while of his prolonged silence she had closed her long eyelids, surrendering to the torpor of the hot morning. This woman brought a frightening agitation to the square logic of his favorite numbers, and this may have been due to his long-term abstinence, his virtually non-existent contact with the other sex, their age difference.

Under the protective shadow of the makeshift awning held by the four stakes, tied to the crossed knots of twine by *Manolis'* experienced hands, on the comfortable embrace of the *chaise longue*, the figure of his wife could tempt any man who came close to her sphere of influence! The idea formed in his mind as he slowly turned his back towards the sea and the turning ship, having reached the height of the big hump of the breakwater, facing again his young henchman at the entrance of the nightclub.

He was so sure that even his henchman would not remain unmoved by the vibrations of this influence, as that behind his back a large ship, with twenty or twenty-five men among the irons and the freshly painted bulwarks, was looking for a safe haven. This certainty again brought to the fore the need to clarify the situation he was in. And just as there was no effective way to limit a beautiful woman's attractions to the men around her, so for him there was nothing capable of stopping him from keeping his eyes open, of finding the end of the thread that would lead him with mathematical precision to the revelation of the hidden truth. He would trap *Nikolas*! The man was honest, he would never lie to him in a question without innuendos, without indirect references—in a single question that would be asked to him so suddenly, like an arrow released from the taut string of the bow quietly finds the target. He would go to find him at the tailor's shop. He drowned in the urge to spin around his heels and start shaking his legs here and now.

And if he did not find him there, he would go to the *café* with the "number seven", where he would surely sit in his usual corner, smoking his cigarette and drinking his coffee. If he had company near him, then he would not have to say much to drive them away. These complete strangers seemed to fear him, and that pleased him deeply. They would leave before he could spin around his heels, closing the *café's* glass door.

The amber rosary swirled so furiously around the tips of his chubby fingers that it made *Maria* open her eyes and move slightly, switching sides on the *chaise longue*. A move that did not go unnoticed by the owner of the *Lido* establishment who had 'his eyes open', his antennae alert. But this, instead of making him stop, pushed him to hit the shiny beads even harder, as if in this way he wanted to hide behind the staccato sound the imperceptible whistle of the released arrow. Yes, *Nikolas* would not lie to him, even in this case in the center of which was his beloved daughter. Sensitive people—and *Michalis* knew very well the tailor from *Kasos* island, his proven sensitivities in family affairs, his seriousness and above all his honesty, his natural aversion to lying—the more serious the issue was, the harder it would be to cover, would adopt a lie to conceal the truth.

The sound of the shiny beads of the amber rosary, a gift from his mother when she returned on one of the many trips his stepfather took her to "not get bored in the monotony of the big restaurant," relaxed and drowned in his fist. He did not want to hurt the creature who, lying in the arms of the hot morning, gave the loose fabric of the sunbed the beauty of shape and the defiant warmth of her magnificent body.

The entrance bell sounded, disturbing the hearing, and *Leilah* appeared at *Manolis'* side. She spoke to him in a low voice, paying absolutely no attention to the couple in the makeshift awning, forcing him to bow his head and lower his arms from his chest. Soon she left him and, retreating, disappeared into the door opening where, before the happy notes were completely subdued, *Manolis* made them heard again following the air left behind by the long dress she was wearing. Tonight she would dance again for the second time after the departure of the 'great *Tarek*'. The first was just last night, when *Michael* was telling her:

'Get ready *Leilah*, today is your day!', pointing with both hands to the crowded hall of the nightclub.

She had danced very well, *Michael* could not fail to admit it, discerning the passion that pulsed in her voice when, addressing especially him with the sweat not yet dried on her skinny body, said to him:

'You don't know how much I enjoyed it, you can't imagine how much I enjoyed this dance tonight Mr. *Michael*!'

She had complained to him two or three times during the two months that the five *Syrian* girls monopolized the elevated dance-stage:

'Let me dance! Do let me dance during breaks, Mr. *Michael*! I can't anymore! I can't bear to see them behind the half-open kitchen door! Please let me, *Michael*!'

He had not taken her seriously and would not let her dance even once while 'the great *Tarek*' was sitting next to him. He did not realize how much *Leilah* had been hurt by this relatively long abstinence from what she knew how to do better than anything else in the world until she thanked him so that even her ugly jaw seemed to beautify behind the passion that was pushing her to do so.

'Thank you! Oh, thank you so much! You don't know how much I enjoyed it, you can't imagine how much I enjoyed this dance tonight Mr. *Michael*!'

In the aura of this strange lucidity, the way details touched him, *Leilah's* emotion had affected him and was stirring him again now with almost the same intensity. Oh, his stepfather and mother had chosen the right people, otherwise it is not explained that for so many years with them he never had the slightest problem. Because it was not only *Leilah* but also *Yusuf* and *Mehmet*! *Mabrouka*, the best cook in the whole of *Alexandria*! And *Manolis*, his young henchman, his own choice, his purely personal choice and the best of all! Yes some people are lucky in life, very lucky. He believed in luck just as he believed in the purity of his numbers, the power of money and his favorite counting. .

In that childish and simplistic "one, two, three, one, two, three!" that kept him company even now that his life had changed. And if luck itself was not something solid, something he could touch if he stretched out his hand, like the earth under his feet or the counting of men sitting in the chairs and resting carefree elbows on the tables of the night-club, *Lido* was a few feet away from him. Low and large, worthy of the kingbirds who flew over the gray canvas of the makeshift awning and who looked from above, majestically turning their heads before deciding to hover away to dive into the hospitable embrace of the sea.

Fifteen

Alexandria, December 1952

A t the pier with the number '12', written in large letters and in red ink on the edge of the concrete dais, more than two hundred people waited patiently to board the passenger ship, high on the crescent moon of the stern of which stood out the name: *'SEA'S EMPEROR'*. The same name appeared further forward and above the round openings, where the black anchors were pulled up to the ship's brow. Three men of the coast guard, staring sternly at the groups of passengers, in front of the stairway and behind the protective ropes, forbade entry to the deck. Despite their strictness, it was obvious that they were telling jokes to each other. It was almost seven in the morning. The ship was scheduled to leave the port of *Alexandria* at this particular time, but for an unknown reason boarding and check-in was delayed.

In the midst of this crowd and having slept a maximum of two or three hours in the last twenty-four hours, he stood alone—just a few meters from the sloping stairway leading to the welcoming deck of the *'SEA'S EMPEROR'*. Without being an exception to that strange anticipation that blended in the fresh air of the harbor, he was incredibly sad because he would leave the city of *Alexander* the *Great* behind him for good. And the alleged reason, constantly aided by the idea that he might return in the future—as a visitor—did not have the power to soothe the extremely unpleasant feeling. But this newfound feeling of anticipation touched him pleasantly.

Like the humming air on his cheeks and breath, dragging along with it and putting aside from time to time the sadness of the impending departure. For he, too, shared what the joyful voices of the children clearly implied—the strange predisposition of the small groups, which fluttered just as loudly in his own soul. It was really strange this contrast, this intensely emotional divergence. It permeated his fatigue like the steady northerly current from the cool lips of the sea, the fabric of his light costume—it gave him the strength to look at the ship with her triple rows of portholes on her sides and twin black funnels in the middle, as if she was a huge white dove, and not just cold metal, painted with the best paints of the trade.

He had hardly slept in the last twenty-four hours because he and his stepfather and mother, 'guests' of the new owner of the *Lido* nightclub, had attended the last performances. *Ismail*, the new owner, had sat at the same table with them without stopping for a moment to speak regardless of what was happening on the illuminated stage.

Being a former sailor, this sixty-year-old *Egyptian* seemed comfortable and perfectly familiar with the world of the night. He still felt sorry, and his sadness seemed to be true, for the old owners of the nightclub.

'It is truly a pity that the local sovereigns no longer permit such undertakings in the hands of foreigners!' he told his stepfather, grasping both his hands with his own, holding them constantly as he spoke to him, looking him in the eye.

And his stepfather said nothing to help him as he lit a cigarette and crossed his arms high on his chest, slowly drawing his gaze towards the half-open kitchen door, where *Leilah's* thin hand held it so she could sneak into the great hall. It was a moment he would not forget in his entire life because, instead of closing it as she always did, she opened it and walked towards their coffee table. She came very slowly to them, as if floating on the sensuality of the oriental music of the six musicians, and her voice, when she finally rested her hands on the limited surface of the table, was so changed! And her aspect too, as if the deep wrinkles on the sucked face had suddenly been removed, hiding her ugly jaw and big nose behind the flashes of her earrings. He could not remember exactly what she said to his stepfather who immediately pulled his hands off his chest and hurriedly extinguished his cigarette, twisting and pressing it back into the full ashtray.

He had stood up immediately, pulling an empty chair, grasping her lightly by the bare arm, but she did not obey his urging to sit down, preferring to disappear again behind the double-leaf kitchen door in the same way she approached them.

They later learned from *Mabruka* that:

'*Leilah* cried for a long time locked up in the small dressing room, keeping her head away from the mirror with the lit lights...'

Leilah, who had found his first stepfather lying prostrate on the wooden floor of his office. His fingers were clenched around a bundle of *Egyptian* pounds—the safe behind his armchair open!

He called *Michael* 'father' when he was younger until one afternoon, speaking sharply to him with his body slightly tilted forward—like a raging bull, ready to surprise and attack, to overwhelm with his colossal strength the unprepared adversary:

'I'm not your father, do you understand, little one? So stop calling me that! My name is *Michael*! *Mi-ha-lis*! Do you understand?'

And, no, he did not understand then, he did not immediately understand, what the little-spoken man, who preferred to let his amber rosary express his feelings, meant. Because this medium of expression was absolutely mute at that moment, confined in his powerful fist. He would have been perhaps ten or twelve years old when the terrible revelation happened, and his mother immediately made sure to explain to him the details of the riddle of his 'father's' unjustified attack. She explained the truth to him with astonishing accuracy, like the spider at the center of the deadly web that warns but also conveys a relentless message to the trapped victim. She even showed him his true father once in the church of *St. Nicholas*. He did not manage, despite his curiosity, to retain anything of his colorless features, nor of the ordinary gray color of his costume. It was as if her finger was pointing somewhere in the void or as if she were pointing at all the men gathered outside the house of God.

Yes, *Leilah* found *Michael* lying in his office. His clenched fingers around the bills indicated that he left doing what he loved more than anything else in this life. The counting and repeated palpation of its power—the power of money, the simplistic affirmation of its power over numbers. This power that found an outlet in the rhythmic beats in the rotations of his amber rosary. He was never mean to him. He may have avoided him, not played with him, shown his displeasure by spinning onto his polished patent leather shoes instead of answering any of his childhood questions, but he was certainly never bad to him. Perhaps... Maybe it was his mother hiding behind it all. His inexplicable behavior, the way he adopted in his interaction with others. But even she would fail to contain true wickedness—if it really existed in her husband's feelings—to touch her child. And secretly, without expressing his feelings, he loved the dark man

He loved his strength, that boundless energy that drove him. The pure power that revealed his own soul, a soul charming despite the simplistic and primitive means of its expression. He admired the way he lit his cigarette. The sleight of hand brought the object to the edges of his lips as if there had been no searching in the pockets of his well-ironed jacket and the box of matches. The little flame was lost for a while in the successive puffs, without extinguishing, until the moment it disappeared into the small rectangular box. He had never been able to see how he was hiding it behind the largest box of cigarettes before both were lost again in the same pocket, prey to the power of the magician. His father, yes, his real father! The little-spoken dark man with the thick mustache and amber rosary, a permanent extension of his feelings projected in his right hand. Because for *Antonis*, *Michalis* was exactly that even after the truth was revealed, even now here at the edge of the crowded pier.

Leilah had stopped dancing several years before the sad event happened and only helped *Mabruka* in the kitchen. An extremely unpleasant situation and in many ways annoying because, as she confided from the beginning to the entire population, male and female, of the nightclub:

'I am born to dance! You hear? I suffer when I see other women up there!'

She had pointed with her free hand—the other holding one leaf of the double-leaf kitchen door half-open—to the place where the notes of the violins started to disperse and reach everyone in the great sala. The thirsty patrons, the glasses that went up and down in their sweaty palms, the tablecloths in the niches of the hundred tables, the creaks in the four hundred chairs, the cloudy air in the semi-dark hall, the insects outside in the illuminated sign that drunken with the blinding light fell one after another on the glass surfaces as if searching in vain, seduced by some cunning and playful spirit, a non-existent way out.

'I'm born to dance, are you listening? I suffer when I see other women up there!' she repeated, turning her head back, looking for the stepson of the nightclub owner for whom she made no secret of her sympathy. A few minutes later, returning from the office of the owner of the *Lido* nightclub where she had gone to see "if he needed anything"—a clean glass or empty his ashtray—it was as if he had met a ghost. The violins fell silent at the news that followed and the great hall was slowly evacuated, under *Manolis'* orders.

The words, in *Arabic*, came out of *Leilah's* lips as if they were passing through the slit in the head of a rusty needle. She nevertheless managed to let the three people in the small kitchen: *Michalis'* stepson, *Mabrouka* and *Manolis*, understand what she could not believe had happened. And the police, who did not take long to arrive, the head of the small group of three constables, quickly came to the conclusion that: "This is not a robbery, and, in all likelihood, criminal activity is excluded since the money was found intact in the safe."

Perhaps the personality of his second stepfather helped in this. The man who lowered his hands from his chest and hurriedly extinguished his cigarette, covering it with the sole of his shoe, every time *Michael* approached him. A tactic that he applied even to young *Anthony* and who, like his great stepfather before him, followed the air swirling behind his mother's dress as if it were an integral part of the lace in the half-dress through which her feet projected like the smelling warps of lilies. And when he once asked him, under the sign of the entrance, having abandoned the crude awning that was set up in the morning and taken down in the evening, when his mother left for home:

'Why do you put out your cigarette every time I approach you? Does this mean anything? Please explain to me!'

He answered him with his melodious voice, a voice that did not contradict at all his general appearance and the way his feet stood firmly on the ground. He explained that he felt comfortable smoking alone or smoking sitting opposite *Giorgio*, the *Italian impresario* and the other agents.

'Not all people are the same, my dear *Anthony*. I think it's very easy to understand what I'm saying, isn't it?'

And, of course, he could comprehend this, he could appreciate the man and understand why he had helped the enemy arrows disappear from the bow of *Michael's* competitors and attract the interest of his beloved mother.

The coroner's verdict was clear: "No sharp object injuries were found anywhere on the body of the owner of the *Lido* nightclub. Nor were traces of poisoning found in his blood..." The dense lines, in the two-page document, mentioned several other technical details that were necessary to properly substantiate the case and concluded as it concluded in the vast majority of cases with the phrase: "His death was due to natural causes and therefore no responsibility is attributed for his unexpected and sudden death."

The strictness of the *Egyptian* authorities obliged at least three close family members to sign the forensic decision to allow the burial of the deceased, and so, in addition to his mother and his own stepson, *Manolis*, his faithful henchman, had signed in place of the third person. *Anthony* remembered him crouching in front of the officer's desk, picking up the pen, and resting his left hand on the edge of the paper on the dull wood of the unkempt desk, where hundreds of other printed documents hid the imperfections of decay and indifference. His mother had signed shortly before, preferring to sit in the only chair that complemented the furnishings of the small room, and there she remained seated until the process was over.

His mother was beautiful. She did not talk much, perhaps because his stepfather did not talk much either, but she was always the focus of attention in their small family.

The first words he remembered from her lips were:

"This house is only temporary, in a short time we will buy a bigger one. It will have a large garden, we will have our own flowers and we will be able to sit in the shade of the trees instead of the shade of the makeshift awning..."

As she spoke, she pointed with her finger outside the large window of their bedroom, towards the sea, where the nightclub was about a thousand steps away. But they never left the small apartment, perhaps because she didn't really want to.

His great stepfather always said that:

'It's so close to *Lido*! We will not find another house that is so close to the sea and so close to work!'

They took him almost every day with them on their morning walks, on the coastal promenade, where the power of the splashes of the waves in the purity of the atmosphere conveyed hidden meanings. He liked to stay a little behind and observe them from a short distance. The seemingly indifferent attitude of his great stepfather could not hide the change in his gait: his legs relaxed at the sound of his rosary, the beads of which seemed to converse more with a strange spirit between the sea and the sky than to express the feelings of his soul. The slight tilt of his head to the side, towards his wife, an attitude entirely different from his usual one—that of the bull in front of the red cloth just before the attack—made him wonder: 'why shouldn't he be his real father?'

But *Leilah* found him lying in his small office. Five years had passed since then, but the scene returned with the clarity of photographic film. *Manolis* had made sure that the hall was quickly evacuated and in the figures of the men, who resented the hasty departure and demanded back the money they gave, he had distinguished the figure of a short man who had burst into the turmoil, for no reason, into a nightmarish and uncontrollable laughter. *Antonis* had asked *Manolis* annoyed:

'Who is this vagabond who respects nothing and dares to laugh in this vulgar way?'

He had seen him chatting with *Michael* shortly before he retired to his office. He was a plasterer from *Mytilene* who, in old age, decided to attend a performance in the nightclub. It is strange that after five full years, this ugly figure of the old man from *Mytilene* came so clearly—like the figures of satyrs in archaic vases that if they could laugh then surely they would laugh in exactly the same way.

And the table knife, which suddenly found itself in *Leilah's* hands, was the result of her terrible irritation, the miserable behavior of the unknown little man.

'I would kill him with my own hands, a minute if he stayed longer in the hall, I would kill him with my own hands!'

Her ugly jaw trembled as if *Enceladus* had suddenly twisted his wounded ribs between her yellowed teeth—the bronze coppers, her favorite earrings, came and went, reflecting the deep wrinkles that grooved her sucked face.

A wrong signal, coming from some children who shouted that:

'The ladder has come down! The ladder went down! Let's get on board! Come on!' caused a temporary disturbance in the countless groups on pier 'number twelve'.

The three coast guards, visibly annoyed by the sudden commotion, looked first towards the reception point at the other end of the sloping stairway, managing to stop the passengers by raising their hands up.

A few feet away, his mother in the center of his small family circle gave him the impression that if she suddenly decided to leave, turning her back on the impatient crowd and the sea, choosing the direction where the *Lido* nightclub was preparing to welcome its first customers, they would follow her without any hesitation. But that was not possible.

His mother had tried hard to take them all with her. "We have a lot of money, enough to buy half of *Durban*!" she told her father many times. She had said the same to *Leilah* and *Mabruka*. But each for different reasons could not fulfill her wish, a desire that certainly found a reflection in their own feelings. *Antonis* understood this too, having explained her plans in detail more than once. He understood that while there was a good chance that he would soon see his grandfather there, at the southernmost tip of *Africa*, this was not the case with *Leilah* and *Mabruka*. And then the *Lido* nightclub, the small apartment by the sea, the thousand steps of distance that *Michalis* had taught her to count on the coastal pedestrian street. All these things of hers would be left behind. She had shown him *Michael's* rosary, carefully pulling it out of her bag. She had asked him looking obliquely, as if defending herself hidden behind the invisible shield that women spread like a spider's web that turns into a mighty weapon in the naivety of the careless: 'Do you want to hold it instead of me?' Her hand seemed to hold something very fragile, something that would scatter into a thousand pieces if handled violently.

In the five years that passed, *Manolis* was able to collect money from the persons who had signed the clean lists of the owner of the *Lido* establishment. By erasing the last name and tearing up the last contract, he had put a dot and a dash on his boss's many years of work. The money, not counting the huge amount of selling the nightclub to the *Egyptian* businessman, was so much that they could easily afford to buy a similar club. A restaurant, say, or even a hotel, why not, ensuring a comfortable life from the start.

His second stepfather and his mother had finally chosen this last resort, and for an additional reason. *Giorgio*, the *Italian impresario*, had managed to convince the former henchman not only because:

'In *Durban* there are very good opportunities for those who make money, eh, *Manolis*!' but also because:

'There are very good friends there, uh, believe me *Manolis*, uh! If I were in your position I wouldn't think about it at all, uh, not at all!'

He had returned from the office of the *Italian impresario*, late one afternoon, determined to convince his wife and *Antonis*.

'*Giorgio* discovered for us an amazing place, "a second America," as he called it! The opportunities are many, too many for those who have money to invest! And, listen to me, *Giorgio* told me that he has friends there, he has people he knows there! Things will be easier for us there, yes, things will be much easier! You know how much I trust *Giorgio*!'

His enthusiasm, however, had not succeeded in fooling either of them, and there was behind the melody of his masculine voice the creeping shadow of a shocking melancholy, which was impossible to mask or disguise. And his second stepfather, the former henchman and for a period of about five years the boss of the *Lido* nightclub, standing a few feet away from him, was a unique figure in the small circle of their familiar group—an exceptional figure in the whole crowd on the pier, in front of the sides of *'SEA'S EMPEROR'*. Near fifty-five years old, he wore black trousers that contrasted with his white shirt. Without a tie and with his sleeves unfastened, raised low on the wrists of his strong hands, he was exactly the man to avoid in a fight. His beautiful face had won over the years, in the perfect proportions of the individual features, in the maturity that almost completely absorbed the slight dullness of the brownish-black eyes. The perfect match against the sweet femininity of his mother, who may have lost the uncontrollable, instinctively aggressive, provocative nature of her youth, but remained always a very beautiful woman.

And like the air coming from the immaculate sea, cool and laden with hidden messages, the former henchman's relationship with his mother. It was first perceived by *Antonis* as the wave of a distant earthquake. And the sound of the amber rosary of the owner of the *Lido* under the crude awning—when it happened that next to *Maria's* lying figure both men were present—as if tuned in to the call of the seagulls' cries, expressed in the most eloquent way what he did not dare to articulate with language. Did the death of his great stepfather have a direct or at least indirect connection with the roles of the 'actors'? *Antonis* could not answer with certainty and doubted, at least, the first hypothesis.

This time the sailor's characteristic whistle at the top of the ladder brought the horn loudspeaker back to face level, to the indifferent lips of the middleman of the trio of coast guards:

'Your attention please! Your attention please! As soon as the ropes are removed, you may start to come on board the ship. Please be extremely careful when you mount the stairway! Do not try to hold each other as you do so! Keep both your hands on the rails and do not stop to look back! Your luggage will soon follow you safely on board! Please do not hurry, and do not push the one who is in front of you...'

The upheaval on the part of the crowd on the pier grew louder from one moment to the next as, while the ropes had been completely removed, no movement could be seen towards the liberated part of the stairway on the side of the *'SEA'S EMPEROR'* vessel. A minute later the first lonely figures were seen climbing the stairs, not looking back for a moment since the voices below did not concern them. But these were few, very few, counted on the fingers of one hand. The vast majority still seemed reluctant. Their indifference was such that it forced the coast guard officer to once again bring the horn loudspeaker to face level and in contact with his jaw:

'You must start to climb the stairway! The ship will depart in less than an hour! Please, ladies and gentlemen, you must come on board at once! We have no time! We have no time!'

But it was as if he was not addressing this people which had their backs turned to the white bulk of the *'SEA'S EMPEROR'*, glancing inwards into the flat earth, at the lights that hugged it like a giant necklace from one end to the other. How would *Michael* be separated, if he lived and was among these people, *Alexandria* and the *Lido* nightclub? He would never find out, and perhaps he was lucky to walk away with his numbers, "my strength," as he liked to say the rare times he approached him to say a word:

'You see, *Tony*, this is my strength, this is the power that will get us to the other side!'

And really his words came true.

'You must start to climb the stairway! The ship will depart in less than an hour! Please, ladies and gentlemen, you must come on board at once! We have no time! We have no time!' the distorted voice insisted.

On the sloping staircase, on the sides of *'SEA'S EMPEROR'*, traffic suddenly began to come alive as the small groups, in concert, replaced the city lights they loved with the brighter lights that adorned the deck of the ship and made her look like a dazzling jewel hanging around the neck of a promising lady. High up in the winter sky, the stars lost none of their glow against the artificial light of the pier and the ornate vessel, the engines of which could be heard in the general noise like a strange echo, like the sound of thousands of sirens that the extremely long distance of these people's destination made sound vaguely threatening.

For more than half an hour the sloping stairway was tried under the heavy steps of the departing stream. A constant current from the moment it started, like a controlled fire that would burn until the end, until it exhausted everything that fed it. *Antonis* embarked late. In front of him his second step-father, the former henchman and last boss of the *Lido* night-club, and in front of him his beloved mother, did not stop once on the steps of the floating stairway as if afraid that if they did they would not have the strength to continue the short ascent to the safety of the hospitable deck. Up there there was a commotion completely different from that on the pier with the number '12'. The letters appeared crystal clear despite the distortion of color under the artificial lighting, and the passengers with their hands resting on the iron rails, as if they had undergone some terrifying metamorphosis, remained motionless, mute, deeply moved.

Leilah suddenly moved to the side of the ship and up the ladder, in an attempt to climb herself, ignoring the strict regulations and the three coast guards. But she did not succeed.

Anthony saw the uniformed officers politely push her back. *Nikolas* grabbed both her hands before pointing up to the spot where the three familiar faces were watching the scene. His stepfather began to shout suddenly, stretching his body, bringing his palms close to his open mouth.

But *Leilah* did not respond to the loud cry that briefly covered the restless silence, incredibly clear and melodic despite the intensity of the moment, nor did she raise her hands to return the greeting of her loved ones. The stepson of the owner of the *Lido* establishment could not distinguish from this height the eyes of the dancer of the nightclub, but he was sure that he saw two sparks flashing there. Two blinding sparks, slightly delayed in succession, resembling the reflection of the great lighthouse of *Alexandria* in the mirrors of the souls left behind. Soon, the *'SEA'S EMPEROR'* would turn on the protective arm of the breakwater, that so familiar breakwater, where his mother used to show him the ships coming and going when she held him on her knees. In the large window of their cozy apartment—just a thousand steps away from the *Lido* nightclub.

Sixteen

Kasos island, January 1953

The flickering of shadows in the light of the oil lamp—resting rather carelessly near the edge on the round kitchen table—the heavy smell of fuel coming to an end at the other end of the wick at the bottom of the small tank, went completely unnoticed as *Nikolas* focused his attention on the coffee heated in the feeble flame of a spirit burner. The natural draught of air prevented the smell of coffee from spreading, but this was a matter that did not cross the mind of the man who, standing in front of the oven, waited with the spoon forgotten between his gouty fingers. The house hid well the bright moonlight, the cold flashes of the stars, and the endless monotony of the night, leaving out what he could not see even if some almighty hand suddenly removed it over his head.

He had journeyed by ferry for many hours to *Agios Nikolaos* and from there for several more until he reached *Frie*. On the almost deserted deck the winter air came at times stronger, and as he touched the wet ropes of the sloping stairway he realized painfully the suspended stillness of the passenger ship, the tickling splashes low, the steady breathing of the sea. This immaculate sea, the power of which he renounced for a quieter life in the vast streets of *Alexandria*. For the sake of the illuminated sidewalks at night, for the charm of the people of the mysterious *metropolis* but also for the charm of the smelly air itself that came to mingle from the depths of the desert with the coolness of the *Mediterranean* in the bustling street markets, to mingle with the safety of solid ground on the worn soles of his dusty shoes. And *Manousos*, standing firmly on the deck of his freshly painted boat, looking imperiously upwards, greeted him heartedly, whispering in his ear:

'Oh my good *Nikolas*, are you traveling alone? Be careful because the sea may be calm, but you don't know when you lose your balance and fall! And at your age it will be pretty bad to break your legs! Come, lo, sit there next to *Minas* ... So, huh, that's it my good man, bravo! Enjoy yourself! You will surely be happy to come back to the island after so many years!'

'Come on, *Nikolas*, here is our island! Do you see it? The same as you left it! Come, sit down my good *Nikolas*?'

He made a slow circular wave with his outstretched hand covering the five villages in the mountains, the few lights in the harbor of *Bouka*, the small lighthouse at the edge of the crude breakwater. The stone breakwater which effectively protected boats and other caiques from the northern winds but did not yet allow large ships to approach and dock safely, as they did in the port of *Rhodes*, say, or in the ports of *Crete* and the large port of *Piraeus*.

'Come on, my good man *Nikolas*! There, *Elias* is waiting for us with his donkey! Come on, let me help you load your stuff! Come! Here is *Elias*! Hey *Elias*, see who came to us from *Alexandria*! Let's help him get home as soon as possible! Are you going to *Arvanitochorio* or *Agia Marina*? Where to, my good man? Just say the word!'

But *Nikolas* had not withheld anything that his compatriot *Manousos* told him at that time and might not even remember that he met him, if he was obliged to answer the question and admit that yes, indeed, he was the one who helped him descend from the ladder of the big ship to the boat and from there to the rocks of *Bouka* last night. *Manousos* who could still tie his boat faster than any other sailor in the entire archipelago, using only one hand—the other would rest behind his back as he liked to do ostentatiously—with safety and unsurpassed skill. The best sailor, the best fisherman in the world! Oh yes, the best of everyone else!

Yes, *Nikolas* might not have been able to remember what *Manousos* told him a few hours before, but other details would come to surface like fish turning their white bellies in the net at the sides of the boat for no reason at all.

His sister had warned him, shaking her head and finger of her raised palm straight before his face:

'*Nikola*, do not ever think of leaving our girl alone on the island! You listen? Do not ever think of leaving her alone a minute on the island!'

It was obvious that she had in mind *Manousos*, the fisherman who would not leave a female at easy, bringing his wife to the edge of despair. His wife, who was one of the most beautiful girls on the island and whom he had stolen when she was sixteen years old, before her family discover them in *Armathia* and marry them on the spot—in the small church of *Panagia* with the priest brought by *Manousos* himself with his boat from neighboring *Karpathos*.

'Ssh...' the brief sound of the sudden extinguishing of the flame around the brass coffee pot in the overflow of coffee, went unnoticed together with the first cries of the roosters. But he could not stand like this, with the spoon between his fingers, and at some point he lowered the coffee pot from the extinguished fire. His hand trembled as he filled the small cup, but he paid no attention to it, nor to the fact that a few drops soiled the floor and the table next to the saucer and oil lamp. The burning from the lit cigarette took over from the oil lamp which after two or three more flashes faded, plunging the small kitchen into darkness.

The owner of the *Lido* nightclub had offered him a cigarette that night. Yes, he had offered him a cigarette, before surprising him by hiding behind his expressionless face. He had taken him by surprise by hiding well behind his well-shaved face, where his thick mustache resembled a warrior's shield ready to hold off not only a soldier but an entire army if necessary, as he lit his own cigarette in the familiar sleight of hand.

'I know it all, *Nikola*! We no longer have to hide behind our fingers! I know it all!'

With these few well-measured words, armed with an articulation that could not be questioned in the slightest, he managed to trap him. He managed to get him to tell the story as he had guessed it and which, despite a nuance here and there, was not far from the truth.

'My nephew mistook the bedroom door... He had a lot of problems with his wife... Many times she resisted him, she would not let him approach her! My nephew drank... He drank a lot! Yes, he drank a lot and... And at some point he did not know what he was doing... Not... He couldn't... He couldn't control himself... My nephew is sick, do you understand *Michael*?'

This confession was strangely easy, as if a priest was opposite him and not the owner of the *Lido* nightclub. His son-in-law, the deceived husband of his beloved daughter. Yes, this confession was unexpectedly easy, perhaps because this time it did not hide the essence, did not negate anything, did not cancel in the slightest the dark act of the drama. And the owner of *Lido* took it so quietly! He did not say a word about what he heard, as if he really knew every detail, leaving the flames in the depth of his half-closed eyes to speak their own language in the broken silence by the beads of his amber rosary.

But in the exasperating 'tack, tack, tack!' in the flutter of nervous spins, it was instantaneously revealed in a way that even the best poets would envy, resentment along with understanding—not only for his *Mary* and his nephew, but for all other characters who starred in the well-staged performance. He had thus remained 'silent', listening for a long time until he lit his next cigarette with that skillful gesture reminiscent of a juggler. Until, after two or three puffs, he said almost without opening his lips through which the smoke was still coming out tuft by tuft:

'Come on, let's have some more wine, my dear friend! Do me a favor to sit until the end, hang out with me tonight. The program is one of the best, believe me, my *Manolis* has taken care of it!'

Yes, he had remained mysteriously 'silent' that night and seeing that the bottle had been emptied he had made a persistent nod with his raised hands to the place where his henchman was waiting standing, causing only awe to anyone who was in the mood for trouble. He did not repeat or add anything else until the second bottle was empty, having let his rosary slip into one of the outer pockets of his jacket, continuing to smoke sparsely his cigarettes as if counting them: 'one, two, three, one, two, three!'

And *Manolis*, the henchman of the *Lido* nightclub, had obeyed by leaning over their coffee table to replace the empty bottle with a full one.

Apart from his mannerly presence, the excellent way in which he put things in order, he did not know in greater depth the beloved henchman of the owner of the *Lido*. Unlike his grandson, he did not realize his passion for his daughter, and, like *Antonis*, he had many unanswered questions in the end. Did the owner of *Lido* know anything about this passion? Had he been fooled by the obedient movements of his beloved henchman? His *Mary* may have exposed him by succumbing to her weaknesses. But *Antonis*, *Michalis'* stepson and *Nikolas'* grandson, had found a worthy and good "second stepfather", as he confided many times under the makeshift awning. In the long pauses of the waves, in the accompaniment of that incessant and ominous 'ssh... ssh!'

'Look, grandpa, mom is coming! And, look, grandpa, next to her...' half a step back in reality, *'Manolis*! What a wonderful man, eh grandpa?'

Yes, there was no question about that, there was absolutely no doubt. *Manolis* was indeed a wonderful man.

And, like the light around the heads of the saints, so in *Nicholas'* wasted mind, these mystical questions had long since lost their power. For he was already over eighty years old and, protected by some divine grace, utterly unable to see the chaos that lay beneath his feet. He had traveled by ferry for no particular reason. A journey he rarely made in the heart of winter even when he was younger, when his children were little kids. It was known to the world that he had three children and the youngest, his son, was embarked on a merchant ship thousands of miles away from *Kasos* island. He had even sent him a letter! A letter, his first letter from 'the *Indies'*, as was written on the exotic and strangely colored envelope next to the postmark and tiny stamp.

'I'm writing to you from *Mumbai*. Here in the distant *Indies* the people is more than flies... The air here is very different from the air of *Kasos*. The air here doesn't even feel like the air of *Egypt*. It's something I can't easily describe in words...'

He wrote to him in a mood of enthusiasm but also laziness because his correspondence was sparse... very sparse! One day he would become a captain, like his ancestors, the pirates, who would not leave the *Turks* and others who happened to pass by their hideouts alone. Captain! Captain yes, but what is the benefit of seeing him for a few days, once every year or every other year? And his correspondence was sparse... very sparse. The boy showed an aptitude for studies, liked to study and read books, and could become a good teacher or a good lawyer, but he did not have the money to study in *Athens*. He had even enrolled for a while in the *'Section* of *Philosophy'* of the *University* of *Athens*, but he dropped out for this very reason—and although his second son-in-law, the former henchman of the *Lido* nightclub, could have helped him financially, he never deigned to ask for his help. Why didn't he dare? But now he was no longer able, not to give a satisfactory answer, but even to grasp the meaning—and if one persisted, the result would be to receive what his age allowed to be projected without any shame.

His second daughter married a merchant from *Cyprus* and saw her, as well as his son, once or twice a year. Unaffected by her husband's "iron discipline," imperious, as he had known her since she was a baby, with his own facial features evident to a much greater extent than in his other children, she seemed to pull the uphill of life as if it were a slide on a playground. She always talked a lot and as if this were a kind of weapon against the silent stubbornness of her *Cypriot* husband, the bursts of her incessant speech diarrhea left no one out. It was impossible for him to imagine her starring in her new role. It was absolutely impossible for him to imagine her walking around with her apron tied tightly to the waist of her elegant body, serving the food she prepared in the kitchen of her new home, bending over the smoke from the tick of the merchant with scanty hair on his shiny skull. That rigid head, tangled between the sheets of the newspaper and the persistent, inquiring eyes of a predator, the same unchanging eyes of an officer in the inspection and punishment.

He was sitting in the tailor's shop, smoking his cigarette and drinking the coffee his assistants had made for him—busy just a few feet away fixing a faulty lining—when he suddenly saw him in front of the counter stretching out his right hand smiling, seeking a handshake with a stranger. In his forties, with the scant hair on his shiny skull showing him at least a decade older. His speech, on the contrary, measured and with a strong island accent, had impressed him with the accuracy of the description and the clear meaning behind the warmth of the vowels. It was, after all, simple and "among men there is no room for shame in such matters!"

'I do not want any dowry, my dear!' he said at one point, just fifteen minutes after they were met—one on one side of the oblong bench and the other on the other.

'The only thing to consider is ... when we get married we will have to leave for *Cyprus*, and that is my only condition!' he continued, hesitating slightly as if he was ready to take back even this one condition in case the man opposite him raised the slightest objection.

But there was no chance of this and his youngest daughter left for *Cyprus* with that merchant, where he practiced his trade and made a lot of money.

'This man looked very dignified, what did he want, master *Nikola*?' his two assistants—*Omar* and *Ishmael*—had asked him in one voice, not stopping to tear off the defective lining on a battered jacket but staring over their glasses, sealing the comical conspiracy against the amiable old man.

'Does he want us to repair him any expensive clothes or sew him a brand new suit, eh master *Nikola*? Well, unless he wants a tailor not just for a dry run but, ha, ha, ha, for as long as he walks on this earth! Eh, master? Ha, ha, ha!'

Nikolas could not share the joy and jokes of his assistants because he did not want another member of his family to leave him—but he joined them, replying that: "Yes, the merchant from the big island wanted a private tailor for life!"

Both of his assistants stood by his side, as is usually the case in the eastern parts of the world where emotion carries more weight than profit and money, supporting the business wholeheartedly. When he was not absent—in the *café* next door—he would sit behind his counter, among the rolls of fabrics, the colorful cords, the scissors and measuring tapes. There, sometimes *Omar's* voice, and sometimes *Ishmael's* voice, reached his ears along with the refreshing sound of hot tea as it poured steadily from the jug into his cup:

'A little more hot tea, master *Nikola*?'

Bending over him, lifting it carefully in front of the trembling fingers, watching him held it to his mouth—where his trimmed mustache still seemed to hold the scepter of an amaranth manliness, the elixir of his youth.

And it may have been true. Yes, it may have been true that he was left alone—but people still loved him! Like his assistants, say, or his compatriot *Manousos*, who along with *Elias* accompanied him, pampering him as if he were a small child, to his family home in *Agia Marina*. He hadn't seen *Elias* for many years, and he seemed so old as he loaded his few luggage on the donkey's back.

'The place is getting deserted, *Nikola*! Young people leave our island like you did, but now things are different! The young people are leaving one after another, they are leaving, and I don't know if they will ever come back!' he told him with his head bowed, looking sideways at him from the loaded animal.

And that too was true. Not that the young people were leaving the island, that did not touch him at all, but that he had grown old and saw himself in *Elias's* figure. An extremely disappointing picture, a look capable of momentarily piercing the iron curtain of past years and completely covering the sad realization of the desolation of the island.

The road to his family home in *Agia Marina* was uphill and they stopped many times along the way to catch their breaths, listening to *Manousos*, who was at least ten feet ahead at each stop, teasing them:

'Okay, I know, you stopped by for *Filomena* to rest! Okay my hearts, let her rest as much as you want because we still have a long way to go, ha, ha, ha!'

The familiar melancholy that engulfed him every time he set foot on the island, was consolidating with every step that brought him closer to the home where he was born. And when his two compatriots walked away, promising to see him again the next day, he felt like he was wrapped in a pitch-black sheet. And *Leilah*? *Leilah* no longer danced. How long was it since he left her? No more than a few weeks. But her ugly face, like the old seer who anticipates the inglorious end, communicating with him in a few words, had managed to move him. Indeed, her words had managed to move him.

'I'd love to see you dance again *Nikola*! I would love to!' she told him on the sidewalk of *Arais Street*, tilting her head slightly to the side, looking him firmly in the eyes as if the whole universe had settled there.

To dance yes, he could still do it now despite the eighty years he carried on his back. To dance with real gusto, the way only he knew how to dance—better than anyone else in the whole world! But now he was far away from *Alexandria* and melancholy plagued him like the pulsating complaint on the mouth of the *Kassian lyre*...

His legs hurt in the joints as, standing in front of the frayed planks of the front door, he turned the iron handle to go out into the courtyard of the house. In the transparent twilight the chapel of *Agia Marina* emerged alive. Lonely and white from the cross at the highest point to the walls low to the ground. Shining even in this scant light, an eternal symbol of faith for those who would come to worship her grace during the long day, she seemed to be preparing for this very reason. Yes, his legs ached in the joints as he walked slowly, for he was over eighty years old, and in his weak mind the shadows of the past came mingled, in no particular order—like fish writhing in the fisherman's net and silvering their tender bellies blindingly in the air. He made his cross three times before bowing reverently. His protruding lips touched the frosted glass, the icon of *Agia Marina*, and, stepping back, he went out again to the small courtyard where he had spent his childhood.